STANDOFF

Fargo squared his shoulders, set his heels, and knocked the riding thong off the Colt's hammer. His features hardened and his voice took on a lethal edge.

"That's mighty tall talk, Lester. A man can turn his tongue into a shovel and dig his own grave."

"You figure you're a killer, huh?" Trilby laid his hand on the butt of his .38 Colt Navy. "I got seven notches in this gun and room for another. So why'n't you two just sashay on outta here afore I perforate your liver?"

"I believe I will," Fargo said.

"Wise man."

"After I kill you," Fargo added, realizing discretion could not save him now. "You just signed your death warrant when you threatened to kill me. Matter fact, if we were under territorial law, you'd be worm fodder by now. So never mind the Indian— *I'm* your daisy. Go ahead and jerk that widow-maker."

THE
TRAILSMAN
#348

BACKWOODS
BRAWL

by

Jon Sharpe

A SIGNET BOOK

SIGNET
Published by New American Library, a division of
Penguin Group (USA) Inc., 375 Hudson Street,
New York, New York 10014, USA
Penguin Group (Canada), 90 Eglinton Avenue East, Suite 700, Toronto,
Ontario M4P 2Y3, Canada (a division of Pearson Penguin Canada Inc.)
Penguin Books Ltd., 80 Strand, London WC2R 0RL, England
Penguin Ireland, 25 St. Stephen's Green, Dublin 2,
Ireland (a division of Penguin Books Ltd.)
Penguin Group (Australia), 250 Camberwell Road, Camberwell, Victoria 3124,
Australia (a division of Pearson Australia Group Pty. Ltd.)
Penguin Books India Pvt. Ltd., 11 Community Centre, Panchsheel Park,
New Delhi - 110 017, India
Penguin Group (NZ), 67 Apollo Drive, Rosedale, North Shore 0632,
New Zealand (a division of Pearson New Zealand Ltd.)
Penguin Books (South Africa) (Pty.) Ltd., 24 Sturdee Avenue,
Rosebank, Johannesburg 2196, South Africa

Penguin Books Ltd., Registered Offices:
80 Strand, London WC2R 0RL, England

First published by Signet, an imprint of New American Library,
a division of Penguin Group (USA) Inc.

First Printing, October 2010
10 9 8 7 6 5 4 3 2 1

The first chapter of this book previously appeared in *Dakota Death Trap,* the three hundred forty-seventh volume in this series.

Copyright © Penguin Group (USA) Inc., 2010
All rights reserved

 REGISTERED TRADEMARK—MARCA REGISTRADA

The Trailsman

Beginnings . . . they bend the tree and they mark the man. Skye Fargo was born when he was eighteen. Terror was his midwife, vengeance his first cry. Killing spawned Skye Fargo, ruthless, cold-blooded murder. Out of the acrid smoke of gunpowder still hanging in the air, he rose, cried out a promise never forgotten.

The Trailsman they began to call him all across the West: searcher, scout, hunter, the man who could see where others only looked, his skills for hire but not his soul, the man who lived each day to the fullest, yet trailed each tomorrow. Skye Fargo, the Trailsman, the seeker who could take the wildness of a land and the wanting of a woman and make them his own.

Northeast Arkansas, 1860—
where the hunter quickly becomes the hunted,
and Skye Fargo discovers that a fish rots from the top.

1

Skye Fargo's Ovaro stallion gave a soft whinny from the stand of pines where Fargo had tethered him.

A *whinny*, Fargo reminded himself, not a trouble whicker. And a soft whinny, at that—the kind he gave Fargo when greeting him in the morning.

Even so, Fargo felt a little tingle of unease.

But the man some called the Trailsman hated like hell to think about stirring his stumps right now. He was sprawled fully clothed in buckskins, up to his neck in the quick-flowing water of a clear sand-bottom creek in northwest Arkansas. The fast current was rinsing some of the trail dust from his clothing. And his legs and lower back were cramped and sore from long hours spent pounding his saddle to answer an urgent summons from Colonel Linton Mackenzie, commanding officer at Fort Bowman.

Fargo had lately been employed as a hunter and scout for a surveying team in the Nebraska Territory when a dispatch rider from the fort caught up with him. Mackenzie's urgency forced Fargo to a pace that had been grueling for man and horse, and they both needed this respite before finishing the last leg south toward the Arkansas River.

Again the Ovaro whinnied—still his soft sound of welcome. Fargo suddenly felt more irritated than alarmed. A whicker would send him up the bank and into the pines, weapons to hand. But a low whinny left him reluctant to move right now—the Ovaro was a reliable bellwether of true danger.

You haven't stayed alive all these years, an inner voice nettled him, *by assuming the best.*

Fargo swore softly, trusting his stallion and lulled by the peace and serenity of this spot. His face was tanned hickory nut brown above the darker brown of his close-cropped beard. De-

1

spite his relaxed state, eyes the pure blue of a mountain lake stayed in constant motion, for unscouted country was the most dangerous. The surrounding slopes were covered with lush green grass, flax, and bright bluebonnets, and the trees were swollen with new sap and budding into leaf.

Now and then his gaze flicked down to the silvery flash-and-dart of minnows all around him. Their swirling patterns lulled the exhausted man, but when the Ovaro whinnied a third time, the sound prodded Fargo quickly to his feet.

You waited too damn long, that survival voice chastised him.

Fargo agreed. He was screened from view by a tall stand of cattails on the opposite bank. Leaving his boots, Arkansas toothpick, and brass-framed Henry rifle on the bank behind him, he shucked his Colt from its holster and waded through the creek.

Fargo slipped around the cattails and up the opposite bank, studying the clutch of trees hiding the Ovaro. Astounded, he glimpsed the back of a man standing beside the Ovaro as he rifled through a saddlebag. Fargo thumb-cocked his single-action revolver and moved closer on cat feet, puzzled at his vigilant stallion's tolerance of a stranger.

"Stand easy, boy," the thief said softly into the Ovaro's ear, scratching his withers. "That's it, just stand easy."

Fargo's curiosity deepened when he realized the intruder was ignoring everything else in the saddle pocket to gaze in wonder at an old envelope. And then it came to Fargo: He knew of only one man who could walk up on the Ovaro . . . a man who could not read but greatly valued discarded envelopes, believing there was strange, potent medicine in white man's calligraphy.

"So, Cranky Man, you still think white man's writing is big magic?"

At the sound of a voice behind him, the intruder leaped like a butt-shot dog. His right hand shot up toward the sheath Fargo knew he wore under the collar of his shirt, behind his neck, producing a bone-handle knife with a blade of shiny black obsidian.

Fargo's Colt bucked in his fist, and Cranky Man's greasy flap hat revolved a half turn on his head. He adjusted it with his free hand.

"Put the knife down and turn around slow," Fargo ordered in a voice that brooked no defiance, "or my next shot will send you to your ancestors."

Cranky Man complied, dropping his knife and turning carefully around to face a grinning Fargo.

"Skye Fargo, you son of thunder! Is it really you?"

"It sure's hell ain't the butter-and-egg man," Fargo said, leathering his shooter.

"Well, punch me in the mug and call me pucker face! I *thought* I recognized that fine stallion."

"Hell, you ought to. The first time we met, you were up to the same foolishness—stealing old envelopes from my saddlebags."

"A bad penny always turns up, eh, Fargo?"

"Bad? Old son, you're corroded. But you saved my life once from border ruffians, and once is enough to make you my friend for life."

The heavyset half-blood Choctaw Indian had evidently fallen on hard times since Fargo last saw him. Beggar's-lice leaped from his clothing, and the weathered grooves of his face aged him beyond his years. He wore torn, beaded moccasins, fringed leggings, and a ratty and torn deerskin shirt adorned with beadwork. Brightly colored magic pebbles depended on a string around his neck.

"Where's your horse?" Fargo asked.

"Tethered in the trees nearby."

"So you jumped the rez again, huh?"

Cranky Man flashed his trademark mirthless grin. "Ain't much of a jump—border's only ten miles west of us. I ain't been back there in three months."

"Why?"

"The tormentin' itch, Fargo, the tormentin' itch. Same thing that drives you. Every now and then a man needs a fresh deck—you said so yourself."

"Horsefeathers. I recall that cave of yours over near Lead Hill, filled with heisted property. Fresh deck, my ass. You're on the dodge."

Cranky Man resorted to a poker face. "Well, now and then a man also needs to take the geographic cure. It'll blow over—I didn't kill a white man or anything like that. What about you—the hell you doing back in Arkansas?"

"I got a message from Colonel Mackenzie, the commander at Fort Bowman. Asked me to get here quick as I could."

"What's on the spit?"

"That's got me treed. I been out in Nebraska Territory. Ain't seen a newspaper in months. But if they sent for me, it'll be low-down, dangerous work a sane man wouldn't take."

"Knowing you, maybe it involves an officer's wife, uh?"

The Choctaw was just being his usual, cynical self. But the remark set Fargo back on his bare heels. "Damn, I never considered that, old son. I *did* have a little fun with a captain's wife last time I was there. Maybe there's a firing squad waiting for me."

Cranky Man howled with mirth. "Serve you right. You never did learn to keep it in your pants."

"And you never learned to put a stopper on your gob."

Cranky Man pulled out his hip flask. "Sheer deviltry makes me this way. Spot of the giant killer?"

Fargo waved it off. "I see you're still chummy with the giggle water."

Cranky Man took a belt and capped the flask. Now his face turned solemn. "My medicine has gone bad, Fargo."

"You're so full of shit your feet are sliding. The only bad medicine you got is that Indian burner in your hand—that poison will ruin you. And if you stick around here much longer, you'll be picking lead out of your sitter."

"I like it here. This is nice country."

"It's pretty," Fargo agreed. "But it ain't Fiddler's Green, you reckless fool. You got the Pukes pouring in from Missouri, Jayhawker gangs from up north in Kansas, and warpath braves from the Indian Territory."

"Like I said, I like it here."

Fargo shook his head. "Well, I might need a man to ride with me on this new job. Interested?"

"I'll face danger, for money, but I refuse to work."

"You ugly red son," Fargo said fondly. "You're lazy as the dickens, but I know you're a good fighter. Fetch your horse."

Cranky Man headed into a thicket of trees while Fargo went back for his boots and the rest of his weapons. Then he returned to his Ovaro and quickly checked girth, bridle, and stirrups before he forked leather. Cranky Man emerged from the trees riding his Indian pony, a dish-faced skewbald wearing a flat, stuffed buffalo-hide saddle.

4

"Where'd you steal that?" Fargo asked, pointing to the New Haven Arms repeating rifle lashed to Cranky Man's saddle.

"From a white man like you who asked too many questions. I'm all right with a long gun out to fifty or sixty yards, but I don't bother to carry a six-gun—I can kill every time with my knife out to handgun range."

"I wouldn't be here if you couldn't. Let's point our bridles south."

The two men emerged from the growth near the creek into an expanse of rugged hills cut with draws and teeming with sweet clover. A china-blue sky showed only a few ragged tatters of cloud, and blackbirds and red-tailed hawks wheeled overhead, wary of these human intruders.

"Yessir," Cranky Man said when they were only fairly started, "this is damn nice country. Peaceful, too."

Just then the Ovaro raised his head, ears pricked, nose quivering.

"Peaceful, huh?" Fargo said.

"For a fact."

"Then you don't know a fact from a hole in your head," Fargo gainsaid. "A graveyard is peaceful, too—we're headed into trouble."

"A life of danger has turned you into a nervous Nellie," Cranky Man scoffed. "This corner of Ark—"

He swallowed the rest of his sentence when a flurry of gunshots, distant but amplified by the hilly terrain, cut him off.

"Let's rustle!" Fargo said, tugging rein and gigging the Ovaro toward the crown of the highest nearby hill even as he speared his brass binoculars from a saddlebag.

A fierce gun battle developed out of sight as both riders climbed the hill. Fargo reached the top first and spotted trouble about two miles below him along bottom country of the Arkansas River. He raised the glasses for a better look as Cranky Man reined in beside him.

"What's wrong?" the Choctaw demanded. "My eyes ain't no good at long distances."

"U.S. Army pay wagon heist," Fargo said, adding in a grim tone: "It's a bloody business, and the gang is damn good at what they're doing."

5

The five bandits had excellent repeating rifles and probably used nearby brushy knolls to gain the element of surprise. The wheel horse hung in the traces mortally wounded and stopping the conveyance. Two of the four soldiers riding guard had managed to unlimber and shoot back, but with the other two, and the civilian shotgun messenger already dead, it was too late to turn the battle.

"They're out of range of your Henry," Cranky Man said.

Fargo nodded, his lips tightly compressed. "They wouldn't even hear it. No point in charging them, either. We'd be two rifles against five, and you can't score hits at distance—those mange pots can shoot. Besides, it's almost too late now."

Even as Fargo said this, a plume of blood erupted from the driver's head and he tumbled off the box of the coach. One of the two remaining soldiers twisted in his saddle, wounded. Armed only with five-shot Spencers, the two beleaguered troopers made the right call and pounded their horses south across the flats toward Fort Bowman.

"Looks like four men are gone-up cases," Fargo told Cranky Man. "The fire was so heavy the two soldiers couldn't even reload. Now two of the gang are breaking into the payroll box with a chisel and a sledgehammer. The others are going after the telegraph wire on the stage road."

Cranky Man said, "Yeah, but I thought soldier blue gets paid in—whatchacallit?"

"U.S. script instead of gold or federal notes. They do. Only soldiers are allowed to spend it."

"Then why do these jaspers want it so bad?"

Fargo kept his glasses leveled on the scene below as he replied. "It's still backed by gold and can be sold in lots, usually for half its face value, to crooked fort sutlers and other merchants who deal with soldiers. They can exchange it for gold and make a fifty percent profit."

"What's fifty percent mean?" Cranky Man asked.

"I'll tell you later," Fargo said, intent on learning every detail he could about the human vultures below. The apparent leader wore flaring leather chaps and a red bandanna over the lower half of his face. The upper half was all in shadow under a wide-brimmed hat pulled low. He rode a blaze-faced sorrel and sat a Texas saddle with a high cantle and horn.

Fargo shifted his glasses to the two men destroying the wire.

"Damn," he said with grudging admiration, "this bunch knows 'B' from a banjo when it comes to crime. One has cut the wire between two poles, but they're not stopping there. He wrapped the end of the wire around his partner's saddle horn, and now his partner's riding way off into the distance, pulling down wire with him. A single cut can be repaired in no time. But this way they'll be days stringing new wire."

"It'll be put on the red man," Cranky Man said, "even though Indians won't touch the singing wires for fear of whiteskin big medicine."

"Not if those soldiers make it back," Fargo said. He watched the blue-green glass insulators pop off the poles like buttons on a fat man's vest as the rider galloped off.

"Now they're all leaving," he said finally. "Riding full chisel off in different directions to confuse trackers. C'mon, old son—let's ride down."

Both riders cantered their horses down the face of the hill and onto the sandy flatland. Fargo knew there was no point in pushing his played-out horse; the gang had tossed finishing shots into the heads of all four men, and even the horses had been killed.

"I don't cry over white men killing white men," Cranky Man said. "But these bastards are just downright evil. They coulda took that soldier money without killing everybody. The hell ever happened to 'throw down your guns'?"

At the scene of the crime, Fargo and Cranky Man put the bodies inside the coach to keep the carrion birds off. Cranky Man was clearly agitated, and Fargo knew it was because of his belief that the soul of a recently killed man could leap into another body.

"Your magic pebbles will protect you," he reminded his friend. "The two men who escaped will send a burial detail back."

Fargo gazed around them, his features etched hard as granite. "Their tracks are clear and we could follow one of these trails. But my Ovaro has been sore-used these last ten days, and he's got a loose shoe—I won't risk laming him. Besides all that, I got orders to report to Colonel Mackenzie. Let's take a quick squint around, then dust our hocks south."

7

Fargo squatted onto his heels and studied the tracks. Usually, in a group of five iron-shod horses, he could find one wearing a flawed shoe. But as if by careful design, all the prints were uniform and unblemished.

"Here's something a mite queer," he finally said. "One of these skunk-bitten coyotes rides a mare."

"How can you tell that from prints?" Cranky Man asked.

"See here where she stood still and pissed behind her legs? A gelding or a stallion couldn't do that."

Fargo was puzzled. Indians would ride a mare, and they were accepted in the land-settled East. But in the rugged West, the bias against them was strong, at least among white men. He stood up.

"Well, the day's still a pup. Let's ride into the fort, and I'll give my report on this."

"I'm damn glad," Cranky Man said, "that we didn't tangle with this bunch."

Fargo grinned wickedly as he swung up into leather. "I wouldn't tack up any bunting just yet, hoss. I got a gut hunch now that I know why Mackenzie sent for me. And that same hunch tells me we *will* be tangling with this bunch."

2

Fort Bowman sat on the south bank of the Arkansas River, with the bustling transportation center of Van Buren just a few miles to the northeast. Fargo estimated the distance between the sun and the horizon.

"I figure we can make it with a couple hours of daylight to spare," he said.

"*We* ain't riding through that gate," Cranky Man said.

"'Course not. Once you jumped the rez you became a hostile."

"The way you say, hair face. I'm always a hostile."

"I hadn't noticed," Fargo said, his tone sarcastic.

The two riders avoided the stage road for fear patrolling soldiers or U.S. marshals might arrest Cranky Man. The terrain was mostly patches of woods interspersed with meadows ablaze with wildflowers, sometimes sliced by gullies washed red with eroded soil. Fargo kept a close eye on the scrub brush at the edge of the timber, a favorite spot for Arkansas's infamous dry-gulchers to lurk.

"How you been staying alive?" Fargo asked his friend.

"Ah, stealing chickens and eggs and such. I scratch up enough to keep the wolf from the door—not that I *have* a door. Usually it's the mouth of a cave."

"Can't say's I blame you for jumping the rez," Fargo said. "Most of the Indian Territory is godforsaken land white people don't want. And the Choctaw sector—hell, it's barren and treeless, and the seeds you plant just blow away when the soil turns into dust."

Cranky Man nodded. "'Rain follows the plow,' my sweet aunt. What drought don't take the grasshoppers do. Sharp Knife Jackson hornswoggled my tribe good."

9

He tucked the reins under his saddle long enough to dig through the chamois pouch on his hip, producing a wrinkled paper sack of the horehound candies he favored with a passion. Fargo had to avert his face so the Choctaw wouldn't see him grinning at what Fargo suspected was coming.

Busy selecting a piece, Cranky Man didn't notice immediately that his skewbald pony had veered toward the timber beside the old game trace they were following. Cranky Man noticed when it was too late.

"Hey!" he shouted, grabbing for the reins. "*Hey*, you loco bastard!"

Cranky Man, Fargo knew from experience, had an extraordinary ability with horses. But he also had a penchant for riding contrary mounts—and the skewbald loved to squeeze through trees that left no room for the rider. Fargo laughed so hard he almost fell from the saddle himself as a low-hanging branch swept Cranky Man unceremoniously off his horse.

"You spavined son of a bitch!" the angry mixed-breed shouted.

"He never runs away," Fargo pointed out.

Cranky Man climbed to his feet, cursing and brushing himself off. "He ain't done this trick in many moons, Fargo. He's showing off for your Ovaro."

"Well, my stallion laughed, all right," Fargo admitted. "Hell, so would a blind mule. For a man that used to be a peeler, you sure got a round ass in the saddle. Now c'mon, let's get a wiggle on. I want to arrive while the headquarters building is still open."

About two miles from Fort Bowman, Fargo found a good campsite next to a seep spring in a copse of pines. There was plenty of graze and a good view in all directions.

"Dig a fire pit," Fargo told his friend. "And soften up some bed ground. I'll leave you some grub, but don't make a fire until after dark. If soldiers see any smoke, they'll be down on you like all wrath."

"You see any green on my antlers?" Cranky Man retorted. "I been giving soldier blue the slip for half my life."

Fargo left him some gnarled hunks of jerked buffalo and a few cold biscuits. Fort Bowman, like most frontier posts, was not walled, and as he rode closer Fargo took in the dreary and disciplined layout in one sweeping glance. Split-log stables, the smithy, the hospital, the enlisted barracks and mess hall lined the left side; officers' quarters, the sutler's store, quartermaster compound and chapel the right. A large parade ground bordered by white-painted rocks lay between them, with the low headquarters building at the head.

And several hundred yards off, isolated but convenient, lay the clapboard hovel called Hog Town, the military tenderloin found near all frontier forts. Never officially sanctioned, Fargo knew these infamous collections of grog shops, whores, and gamblers were necessary to keep down desertion rates—the greatest enemy of a soldier was boredom.

Fargo reined in at the tie-rail in front of headquarters and swung down, his body weary and sore. He wrapped his reins around the rail and then slipped the bit and loosened the cinch. By the time he was ready to go inside, a small ring of cavalry soldiers in high-topped riding boots had formed around him. Fargo took in their sullen, hostile faces.

"I take it you boys ain't too happy to see me," he remarked.

"You're Skye Fargo," said a husky sergeant tanned almost as brown as Fargo. "You hear about the payroll heist today?"

"I haven't heard about it," Fargo replied, "but I saw most of it."

"I'll just bet you did," said a carrot-haired private.

"I saw it through field glasses," Fargo clarified. "I was too far away to do anything about it. I plan to give a report to Colonel Mackenzie."

The sergeant's mouth firmed. "That dog won't hunt," he said. "You were part of that holdup."

"Where did you get *that* little sugarplum?"

"Witnesses to other holdups lately have seen a tall man with a beard, dressed in buckskins and astride a black-and-white pinto."

"Witnesses, huh? Name one of them."

"Well . . ." The sergeant momentarily lost his bluster.

"He just come here to cover his ass, Sergeant Manning," carrottop insisted. "He's a murdering son of a bitch. He saw it, like hell. I say we ought to settle his hash right now before the old man can protect him."

Fargo didn't normally suffer insults and slanders from strangers, but soldiers were more like remote kin to him. Besides, more than most men they were exposed to vicious rumors that became "facts" by sheer repetition. His wisest course, he realized, was to endure their calumnies and clear this damn mess up.

"You are all mighty mistaken," he told them. "Around forts, rumors are thicker than toadstools after a hard rain—hell, you fellows know that."

He met each man's eye, some of them averting their gazes. "I'm looking around, boys, and I see the faces of men I rode with. You, Corporal Lofley—that time up in the Dakota Badlands, when the Sioux had your squad surrounded, did I fall back when Lieutenant Hartley had the bugler sound retreat?"

"No, Mr. Fargo, for a fact you did not," said a noncom with a livid scar on his left cheek. "You rode right into the Sioux and made them so mad they all chased you while we escaped. Your stallion outrun 'em, but you took an arrow in your back."

"Damn straight. The contract surgeon pulled the shaft out, but the point is still in me—I feel it in fog or rain. Now, why in hell would a man take that kind of risk for soldiers, then turn around and murder them in cold blood? I was only a scout, not a fighter."

"It don't cipher," Sergeant Manning admitted, looking less bellicose.

"Besides, look at me, boys. Worn-out buckskins, worn-out boots, a hat with bullet holes in it—would *you* look like this if you had a mountain of stolen script?"

"I never believed you were in on it, Mr. Fargo," Corporal Lofley insisted. "I came along with these gazabos so I could help you when the fight broke out."

"The *fight*," Fargo said, "started when I watched four men get murdered today in cold blood and couldn't do a damn thing about it. You boys just hold your whist—come hell or high water, there *will* be a reckoning."

"Fargo," Colonel Linton Mackenzie said in a solemn voice, "this area is settling up rapidly, but with more population comes more outlaws. The War Department is adamant that these highwaymen be brought to justice swiftly. We've had two attacks on pay wagons and the seizure of a weapons shipment. I've lost nine men, and eight civilian contract workers have been killed. We have a good, honest U.S. marshal in Van Buren, but frankly, he's my age, and this job calls for a strong young buck like you with exceptional trail skills."

Mackenzie was a stern-visaged, silver-haired man around fifty years old. His campaign hat with the yellow cavalry cord rested on his desk. Known as Old Fuss and Feathers by his men, he rarely commanded in the field, but Fargo knew he had been a capable battle leader as a field-grade officer.

"From what I saw today," Fargo said, "this gang is well led and plans their attacks down to the last detail."

"Precisely. These are not just stupid stumblebums—they're heist artists. They succeed every time and rarely leave a witness."

Mackenzie scraped back his chair and rose to his feet, clasping his hands behind his back and pacing in front of a large wall map of Arkansas and the adjoining Indian Territory.

"Naturally I've sent out patrols," he said. "But you know how it is with soldiers—we have to hire men like you to do any real scouting and tracking. Besides, I've got enough on my plate as it is. You may have heard there's been yet another cut in the Indian annuities, and they're already on short rations. So every week we get a new bust out from the eastern sector of the Indian Territory, and this is the closest fort."

Mackenzie's direct, nimbus-gray eyes bored into the Trailsman. "Fargo, I'll be blunt. A man who spends too much time alone doesn't think like the majority. Often that's good. But, other times, being a bunch-quitter makes a man reluctant to follow orders. This is no job for a one-man outfit that answers to no authority—do you understand?"

"Colonel, you make it sound like I'm a hermit living in a cave. I've taken plenty of orders from the army."

"True, and ignored plenty, too. Well, I don't want to be a brake on your initiative. As one philosopher put it: 'A man more right than his neighbors constitutes a majority of one.' But I want your solemn oath that this will be nothing but a scouting mission."

Fargo shook his head. "I don't take oaths. But you have my cast-iron guarantee I'll do my best to follow orders."

"Skye Fargo's word rates high with me." Mackenzie mulled something for a few seconds. "Son, how'd you like to take up residence in a small town for a while?"

"Frankly, Colonel, I'd rather buy ready-to-wear boots."

"The pay is five dollars a day and a generous per diem."

Fargo debated the offer. The rattle and hullabaloo of cities, even small ones, grated on his nerves. But in a small town, the wide-open spaces were never far away, and the press of humanity easier to bear. Especially the female portion of it.

"Just call me a board-walker," Fargo finally replied.

"Good man. But when I say 'small,' I don't mean peaceful. Have you heard of Pine Hollow?"

"Due south of here, innit?"

Mackenzie nodded. "Pine Hollow isn't one of those born-on-the-spot towns like you'll find out in the territories. There's families living there, a school, a church. Oh, they still use the saloon for a courthouse and there's gunfights now and again. But Sheriff Cody Jeffries keeps most of the rough stuff tamped down."

"Colonel, no offense, but this is Arkansas, not Vermont. I've had some of my roughest scrapes here. If there's a peaceful town anywhere in the state, I never heard of it."

"Well, I can't deny the state is wild and woolly," Mackenzie admitted. "But the town itself is relatively calm thanks to Sheriff Jeffries. Before he was elected, the place was called Hangtown."

"Yeah, but you just admitted the town isn't peaceful."

"Yes, but that's only because the region beyond Sheriff Jeffries's jurisdiction has become a heller. Outlaws on the dodge, marauding redskins, gunrunners, whiskey smugglers . . . my troops patrol, but the fort is seriously undermanned—the entire frontier army is barely holding the line. I can hardly put three squads in the field."

Fargo nodded. "But why Pine Hollow?"

"I've plotted out the attacks on the map. The tracks we've been able to find eventually lead toward that region. More to the point—there's a clan, the Ravenel family, who own a farm near Pine Hollow. There are three hotheaded brothers who have unsavory reputations as gunrunners and smugglers."

"Any evidence they're part of the gang?"

Mackenzie shook his head. "Just circumstantial. Eyewitnesses have placed them near one of the robberies."

"According to some of your men," Fargo pointed out, "*I'm* in the gang."

The colonel waved this aside. "That rumor no doubt originated in Hog Town. Nobody takes that horseshit seriously."

Fargo begged to differ but held his tongue.

"Skye, I need to make one point clear. A man as smart as you requires reminding more than instructing. Arkansas is a state, whereas you spend most of your time in the territories. Too much . . . violent interference on your part could embarrass the U.S. Army—or worse. I'm hoping to replace these eagles with stars."

"When a colonel calls me smart, naturally I worry. No need to take the long way around the barn—just give me the straight."

"I mean that we must sift this matter to the bottom, but discreetly. You're just going to Pine Hollow to get a scent. None of this business like you pulled in the Sweetwater Valley recently, acting as sheriff, judge, and executioner. All I require of you are reports to be sent by dispatch rider. Well, that's the situation and the box it came in—are you still on board?"

"It's all jake by me, Colonel. I like coffee-cooling details."

"Excellent." The colonel sat down at his desk. "Basically, Fargo, I want you to take it easy for a spell. In addition to your pay, as I mentioned, you'll receive per diem. Drinking, gambling, whoring to your heart's content, all to be paid for by the War Department. Try not to abuse the per diem."

Fargo's lips twitched into a grin. "That sounds like you're promoting me to a general."

Mackenzie smiled, the first time since Fargo had arrived. "I'll call that humorous until I make my first star. The point is that I want you in town, Fargo. If you can, take a room above the Razorback Saloon. The Ravenels have a sister who works there as a dime-a-dance girl. You have a certain reputation for . . . charming the ladies."

Fargo grinned. "Is that what it's called now?"

"Call it what you will, but draw her out. Her brothers also frequent the saloon, so put your famous powers of observation on them, too."

"Sounds to me," Fargo said, "like you have nobody else in mind but these Ravenels."

"Well, Sheriff Jeffries is suspicious of them, but of course you'll be observing everyone. Fargo, you're no halfway man. But this time you must haul back on the reins. I can't deputize

15

you, and this is a federal matter requiring federal prosecution. Just determine the lay of things—as I said, get a scent."

Fargo pushed to his feet and shook the colonel's hand. But "hauling back on the reins" didn't fit his present mood. The memory of what he'd seen earlier that day already had a scent—the foul stench of cold-blooded murder.

Fargo rarely traveled after dark if he could avoid it, and the sun was a dull orange ball on the western horizon when he rode out of Fort Bowman. He joined Cranky Man at the campsite north of the fort and set out for Pine Hollow, several hours ride due south, right after sunup.

"Maybe we should part ways," Cranky Man said soon after they set out. "Riding into town with an Indian ain't exactly the best way for you to make friends."

"Yeah, I thought about that. But your old man was white, and breeds are better tolerated. Besides, we're both going to lay low until I see which way the wind sets."

Cranky Man snorted. "My sweet aunt! *You*, lay low? Fargo, you're a caution to screech owls. The minute you arrive any-place, hell's a-poppin'.."

"Yep, you prove there's a joker in every deck," Fargo said amiably. Cranky Man's quarrelsome nature didn't faze Fargo a bit. It disguised a brave and loyal friend with impressive fighting skills. From what Fargo had seen of that gang, he'd need just such a friend before this was over.

"Keep your eyes skinned," Fargo remarked. "Border ruffians like this corner of the state, and with reservation Indians on the scrap, things could get lively in a hurry."

The terrain hereabouts varied widely, from pine flats to rugged hills with boulder-strewn draws and narrow gulches. While Fargo didn't find it as daunting as the salt deserts and lava-rock canyons of the Far West, it was excellent ambush country—especially considering that the vast Indian Territory began only ten miles to the west. And few Indians, in Fargo's experience, cared spit about boundaries drawn on maps. Cranky Man proved that.

"The thing I don't get," Cranky Man said, "is why them soldiers think you're in the gang. Hell, you been working for Uncle Whiskers for years and never stole a dime—or did you?"

"The colonel figures the rumor got started in Hog Town."

"But who woulda started it?"

Fargo shrugged one shoulder. "Where do elephants go to die? I've made plenty of enemies over the years. Might've been a gambler—I've fleeced a few."

Soon the terrain grew less formidable, leveling out to sparse woods and shaded meadows. A few scattered stump farms dotted the area, none very prosperous and most, Fargo guessed, occupied by squatters.

They drew abreast of a wind-scrubbed knoll crowned by a huge boulder. Fargo tugged rein and veered off the trace.

"Let's spell the horses," he said, swinging down from the saddle. "I want to take a good squint around."

He loosed the cinch and threw the bridle. Both men filled their hats from a goatskin bag of water lashed behind Fargo's cantle and watered their horses.

"Yeah, suck it down, bastard," Cranky Man growled at his skewbald. "Next time you knock me on my ass, you're going to a rendering plant."

Fargo took his field glasses and climbed the knoll, perching on the crown of the boulder. He studied the landscape in all directions.

"Spot any trouble?" Cranky Man called up to him.

"Looks peaceful. A couple punkin rollers out working their fields, is all. I can see Pine Hollow, too, but only the top of it. It's down in a little hollow, all right, in the lee of a rock slope on its south side."

A half hour later they entered town from the west, their trotting horses kicking up yellow plumes of dust. It was a bustling place with new buildings of milled lumber, boardwalks along Main Street, and a three-story hotel with a green wooden awning and a row of iron palings out front. The false fronts along Main Street suggested that a mere crossroads settlement was becoming a prosperous town.

"Looks to be booming," Fargo said.

"The undertaker's parlor will be," Cranky Man replied, "now that you're here."

"And maybe you'll fill his next pine box."

A steep slope bordered Pine Hollow on their right, and a rock dike held back the loose talus slope. But not everything supported Colonel Mackenzie's description of a law-and-order town—they rode past a dance hall with the windows boarded up.

"Too many fights," Fargo surmised. "Dance halls don't last long west of the Mississippi."

The usual town loafers, backs supported by buildings and eyes lidded, watched them ride in. Among the masculine throng on the boardwalks, Fargo even spotted a few women in calico dresses and gray sunbonnets.

The Trailsman was pleased to find a clean and prosperous-looking feed stable at the end of the street. Several horses in the paddock were enjoying a roll in manure. The two men veered into the hoof-packed yard, and Fargo suddenly hauled back on the reins, not believing his eyes.

"Great jumping Judas," he muttered to Cranky Man. "Do you see what I see?"

3

Skye Fargo was no novice when it came to judging woman flesh. And he judged the lass he was looking at now as right at the top of the heap.

"Lick your chops all you want to," Cranky Man muttered as the two men dismounted and led their horses closer. "That's one juicy little morsel you'll never taste. *Never*, Fargo, not even you."

The woman had striking, nutshell-shaped eyes, and her wheat-blond hair was pulled into a twist under a gaily beribboned straw hat. She wore an expensive, exquisitely tailored riding habit—flattering her ample breasts and the taut half globes of her high-split rear—and soft kid boots. She stood, riding crop in hand, while a young black man led a fine-looking chestnut mare with white front socks toward the upping block used by women and children.

"That's a sidesaddle," Cranky Man said. "That mare's been lady-broke. I thought western women rode straddle like men?"

"Not if they learned to ride back east," Fargo said, watching the woman gracefully mount. His gaze drinking her in, he felt a stab of loin heat.

Cranky Man, watching Fargo size her up, chuckled. "You grin any wider, you'll rip your cheeks. So she's the meat and you figure you're the tiger, uh? And tomorrow the sun will rise in the west. I'm telling you, Fargo, you've met one who won't fall."

The woman wheeled her mare and headed right at the two men. Fargo quickly knocked the trail dust from his hat and speared his fingers through his hair. She reined to a stop and gave him a look he couldn't decipher before quickly dismissing him. She shifted her gaze to Cranky Man and eyed him with cool distaste.

Fargo tipped his hat. "Good afternoon, ma'am."

"I don't converse with trail trash," she replied, the scornful twist of her mouth making it clear she saw herself as a frontier princess. "I only stared at you two because I wondered if there's a freak show in town."

Fargo's jaw went slack with surprise at her peppery retort, but he quickly recovered and flashed his strong white teeth in a grin. "I favor skipping the conversation, too," he assured her.

If she caught his drift, she didn't let on. "Sir," she told Fargo with icy hauteur, "there's a bathhouse behind the hotel. My nose tells me you both should go there."

"I'll take that under advisement," Fargo said. "I am a mite ripe."

She gigged her horse past them and Cranky Man chortled. "Hah! Snip-snip. The lady killer just got gelded."

"She's an ice queen," Fargo admitted. "But ice thaws."

"Are you loco, hair face? They'll get holidays in hell before you get under *her* petticoats."

"Care to place odds on that?"

Cranky Man's thumb and forefinger massaged the point of his chin. "Nope. Not with a man who combs pussy hair out of his teeth."

Fargo watched the beauty head west out of town. It struck him as risky for a woman to ride without a chaperone—especially one that comely. For a woman who played the great eastern lady, she sure didn't mind dropping the chaperone rule.

"I'll tell you, old son, trying to figure out a woman's mind is like trying to bite your own teeth."

The liveryman approached the new arrivals. His brown eyes cracked deep at the corners when he flashed them a broad, gap-toothed grin. "Hep you gen'muns? Dolomite Jones is the name."

"I'm Fargo and this ugly mutt with me is Cranky Man." Fargo hooked a thumb toward the retreating woman. "I'd wager that cottontail has no rival hereabouts for all-out bitchery, Dolomite."

Dolomite looked carefully around. "I know *that's* real. Miz Felicity sure doan live up to her name. That woman *mean*."

Dolomite turned his attention to the Ovaro, and his face perked up. With a well-trained eye he examined the pinto's impressive muscle conformation and powerful haunches.

"Great day in the mornin'! I been running this livery since my owner freed me five years ago, and this here is the finest horse I ever did see. This here paint puts an Appaloosa in the shade, Mr. Fargo, for a fack he does."

"He'll do to take along," Fargo agreed. "How 'bout a feed and a rubdown for both horses, to start with?"

"Awright."

"Got room to board them?" Fargo asked.

"Yessir. Four bits a day for the pair."

Fargo nodded. "When you get a chance, Dolomite, would you trim my stallion's feet and nail the rear offside shoe on tighter? It's starting to click. He won't kick once he knows you."

"No trouble a-tall. Me 'n' horses gets along like syrup and hotcakes."

Fargo and Cranky Man handed the liveryman their reins.

"Say, Dolomite," Fargo added, "would you be interested in an extra two bits a night to let Cranky Man sleep in your hayloft? It's a cinch bet the hotel won't take him."

Dolomite laughed. "Shoo, this town won't even hire an Indian to catch rats. Some been shot on sight for target practice. Course you can stay, Mr. Cranky Man, and forget the two bits. Us colored mens got to stick together."

Cranky Man scowled and opened his mouth to protest, but Fargo jabbed an elbow into his ribs.

"Much obliged," Fargo said.

Dolomite started to lead the horses into the livery barn, then stopped and looked back at the men. "Fargo . . . a fine pinto stallion . . . beard and buckskins. Moses on the mountain! Sir, is you Mr. Skye Fargo—the gent some calls the Trailsman?"

"That would be me, for my sins."

Dolomite slapped his thigh. "I be hog-tied and ear-marked! I hear fellows talkin' about you from time to time."

"Especially lately, right? Rumors that I'm part of a holdup gang?"

"Yessir, but ain't many folks credit that story."

"Well, I'd appreciate it," Fargo said, "if you'd keep my name quiet. I'm here for a rest, and I'd like to avoid any stirring and to-do."

"Sorry to hear that," Dolomite said. "I been hopin' somebody would ride in and scrub this town clean."

Fargo's eyes narrowed. "I was told it's already pretty clean."

"Nuh-un. Mr. Fargo, this town goin' to hell on a fast horse, my hand to God. Good folks bein' run out by bad, and bad money chasin' out good money."

"I was also told the sheriff is honest."

Dolomite turned away. "Ain't my way to talk 'gainst white folks."

"Why not?" Cranky Man intervened. "I sure's hell do. These peckerwoods don't scare me."

"Well, they scares *me*. I can tell you're half white, but I ain't."

"This doesn't go past me and you, Dolomite," Fargo promised. "Is the sheriff crooked?"

Dolomite took a careful glance around before speaking. "Cody Jeffries been kind to me. Even helped me set up this livery. He ain't no badge-happy bully, and he don't go pokin' into people's business. He a good-natured man with a kind word for ever'body."

"All right," Fargo said. "But do you think he's crooked?"

"I never seen proof he crooked, Mr. Fargo. Never. But they's times when he don't poke in people's business enough. And the man sometimes be friendly with men would shoot they own granny for a plug nickel. 'Course, Cody Jeffries be a mighty friendly man to ever'body. Uh-oh, look out."

Fargo heard a horse whinny and glanced behind him. A heavy-set, pig-eyed man astride a big sorrel was staring at Cranky Man.

"Watch this one," Dolomite muttered. "Lester Trilby. He mean as a snake."

Fargo sent Cranky Man the high sign to keep quiet, but the Choctaw ignored it. "What's bitin' on you?" he asked the man on horseback. "You never seen a red Arab before?"

"Bad enough," Trilby growled, "we got to let darkies stare at our wimmin'. I ain't having no goddamn mouthy savage in Pine Hollow."

"He's with me," Fargo said in an amiable tone, recalling Colonel Mackenzie's orders not to stand out on this information-gathering mission.

"That don't signify, Indian lover. He ain't one of ourn. Leastways, Sambo here has got legal papers and knows his place. This gut-eating savage has jumped the rez. That's agin the law."

"If I was a gut-eater, you cracker blowhard," Cranky Man spoke up, "that belly of yours would feed me for a year."

Trilby's lips eased apart in a sneer, revealing teeth stained brown from tobacco. "Who you tryin' to fool, breed? You couldn't break an egg with a hammer. Like I said, you're breaking the law. I could cut you down right now and leave this nig to bury you."

Fargo elbowed Cranky Man silent, worried about that knife behind the Choctaw's neck. If Cranky Man killed this fool, which he easily could, it would ruin Fargo's mission.

"Look, friend," Fargo reasoned, "there's laws being broke all over this state. What about the whores and the moonshine and the tax dodgers? I'll bet you don't bellyache about none of that. Maybe you just got a pinecone lodged up your sitter."

"They always talk who never think. Stranger, you're dancin' on dynamite. You best pack up this red sweetheart of yours and haul him back to the rez pretty pronto afore I send both of you over the River Jordan."

Fargo squared his shoulders, set his heels, and knocked the riding thong off the Colt's hammer. His features hardened and his voice took on a lethal edge.

"That's mighty tall talk, Lester. A man can turn his tongue into a shovel and dig his own grave."

"You figure you're a killer, huh?" Trilby laid his hand on the butt of his .38 Colt Navy. "Mebbe the darkie here ain't told you who I am. I got seven notches in this gun and room for another. So why'n't you two just sashay on outta here afore I perforate your liver?"

"I believe I will leave," Fargo said.

"Wise man."

"After I kill you," Fargo added, realizing discretion could not save him now. "You just signed your death warrant when you threatened to kill me. Matter fact, if we were under territorial law, you'd be worm fodder by now. So never mind the Indian— *I'm* your daisy. Go ahead and jerk that widow-maker."

The sea change in Fargo's manner and voice took the bully by surprise. He gave the Trailsman a good size-up and lost some of his bluster. "You know my name, but I didn't catch yours."

"That's because I didn't throw it. It's Fargo."

"Far—?" Trilby paled noticeably. "Them things I said about killing—it was just a manner of speaking, Mr. Fargo."

The last thing Fargo wanted was to announce his arrival in town by killing a man. "That's jake by me, especially since you were just leaving."

Trilby did just that, reining his horse around and heading back out of town at a gallop.

"Welcome to Pine Hollow, Mr. Fargo," Dolomite said.

"Yeah," Fargo replied. "A real law-and-order place."

With the afternoon shadows starting to lengthen, Fargo left Cranky Man at the livery and set out to make a quick inspection of Pine Hollow. He treated towns no differently than he did the wide-open spaces: both should be scouted in case trouble struck. There were escape routes to learn, ambush spots to avoid.

He strolled west to east, noting a couple of alleys that might prove useful. The one side street, running north to south, had only rammed-earth sidewalks, but, like Main Street, had been ditched. As he returned to Main Street, an undertaker in a tall plug hat emerged from his parlor. He sized Fargo up with an expert eye and rubbed his hands together briskly.

"Ah, business is about to pick up," he said in a cheerful voice at odds with his cadaverous face. "Artemius Ward is the name, sir, and for each dearly departed you send my way there's a two-dollar bonus in it for you."

"I reckon that's more bounty than I can expect from a buzzard," Fargo said, shouldering past the ghoulish corpse collector.

Of the three saloons in town, the Razorback, mentioned by Colonel Mackenzie, was clearly the most prosperous. Fargo glanced over the top of the slatted batwings and saw that the place was doing a land-office business thanks, in part, to the wide selection of gals topside, openly advertised in gilt letters near the door.

A competitor saloon, the Stardust Tavern, was less prosperous and catered to the tattered and tough. Fargo watched a fist-fight spill out into the street and turn into a boring wrestling match.

Fargo walked up to the Razorback, brushed the batwings inward, and stepped into a cavernous emporium sporting a long, burled walnut bar with a brass rail. A barkeep in vest and sleeve garters, his hair plastered straight back with axle grease, wiped up beer slops with a rag. A sawdust-covered dance floor took up the west end of the building, and there was even a starling in a wooden cage to add a touch of big-city elegance. Fargo noticed, however, that the NO ROUGHHOUSING sign behind the bar had been penetrated by several bullets.

"What's yours?" the barkeep greeted him.

"Give me a beer, wouldja? And draw it nappy."

"Your business is welcome, stranger, but I always notify new customers that I can accept only gold or silver coins—no State Bank Notes."

"Can't say's I blame you, bottles. I don't trust money that wrinkles."

Fargo flipped a silver dime onto the counter and cut the trail dust by quaffing half the beer in two gulps.

"Case you're in a sporting mood," the barkeep said, "we got six gals upstairs. Each one checked by a doc once a week."

"Maybe later," Fargo said. He moved to a centrally located table where he could observe the saloon's occupants better. A piano player and a fiddler were giving a lively rendition of "The Blue Tail Fly" while a half dozen or so dime-a-dance girls whirled around the floor with male patrons.

Dolomite Jones had confirmed that several rooms were for let above the Razorback. Colonel Mackenzie had urged him to take one, pointing out that a dime-a-dance girl named Jessie Ravenel worked there—a sister of the men Mackenzie suspected in the holdups. But Fargo wanted to con the situation over first. He had just experienced, yesterday at Fort Bowman, what it was like to be the victim of a rumor.

He studied the girls, and almost immediately one stood out from the rest: a petite, shapely gal with cheeks like fall apples and long, chestnut hair worn in a braid over her right shoulder. She wore a blue gingham dress, simple but pretty and quite flattering to her womanly form.

"Hey, you two sissy-boys!" a florid-faced man two tables over shouted in a truculent voice to the musicians. "Play 'Dixie's Land' or I'll smash the pianer to kindling!"

The duo hastily complied while the bully pushed unsteadily to his feet. The loudmouth had a self-satisfied smirk that irked Fargo.

"Take it easy, Butch," cautioned a younger man who was almost a replica of the blowhard. "There's quiff upstairs."

"In a pig's ass! Ain't nothing as good as that Ravenel bitch," Butch assured him. "I'm gonna rub her up good."

It was the third man at their table, however, whom Fargo instantly pegged as the most dangerous: a sunburned, furtive-looking man thin as a winter aspen. He had the lean and hungry look of a casual killer. All three men wore vicious spade bits, the kind that tore a horse's flanks—and the kind favored by outlaws to force bursts of speed from their mounts.

Fargo sensed trouble coming and resolved to honor Colonel Mackenzie's order: *We must sift this matter to the bottom, but discreetly. You're just going to Pine Hollow to get a scent.*

The Trailsman watched Butch's huge bulk stagger out onto the dance floor. With one casual swipe of his left arm he sent the Ravenel girl's dance partner, a middle-aged farmer in bib overalls, stumbling to one side. He pulled the girl close in a crushing hug and, not even bothering to dance, began sampling her body with his hands.

Fargo watched red splotches of anger leap into her cheeks. But when she tried to slap him, Butch caught her by the wrist.

"I *like* a feisty bitch," he said in a drunken voice that carried over the music. "Them's the kind what crawl all over you in the sack."

She aimed a defiant stare at him. "Keep your cooties off me, Butch Sloan. There's gals upstairs for what you want."

Butch glanced over at his two companions and gave an exaggerated wink. "Brash as a government mule, ain't she?"

He looked back at the girl, his mouth set mean. "A whore is a whore whether she's upstairs or down, Jessie. You charge a dime a dance, so here's two bits for your quim. I expect change back if it ain't top-notch."

She slapped his hand so hard that the quarter flew into the back wall. Butch swore and backhanded her, and Fargo flew up from his chair, crossing the floor in a few lengthy strides. But he still had Mackenzie's order in mind.

"Excuse me, sir," he said amiably. "I'd like to cut in."

Butch Sloan's drunken eyes traveled Fargo's considerable length. "Well, Jesus K.T. Christ! It's Caleb Green the mountain man! Where'd you leave your Hawken rifle, shit heel?"

"There's no call for insults. Nor for hitting this lady."

"Shut your piehole, buttinsky. If I want your opinion, I'll beat it out of you."

By now Jessie Ravenel had squirmed out of Butch's grip and taken refuge behind Fargo. Butch's apparent younger brother came to his brother's side.

"Don't let his size snow you, Butch," he said, mocking Fargo with a sneer. "These 'gentlemen' are all wood and no sap. When it comes down to the nut-cuttin' they run like a river when the snow melts."

The new arrival made the mistake of grabbing Fargo's shoulder. Fargo could abide a few insults, strictly in the line of duty, but he never tolerated being laid a hand upon. He lifted the miscreant clean off the floor with a solid haymaker, sending the man's hat flying. His knees came unhinged and he dropped to the sawdust-covered floor like a sack of dirt.

Butch Sloan slapped leather, but Fargo's Colt seemed to leap into his fist. He quickly thumb-cocked the weapon. The music suddenly stopped, and the crowd parted like the Red Sea. Sloan froze with his hand on the butt of his Remington.

Fargo kept the corner of one eye on the third man, but he kept his hands on the table and showed little interest in this barroom set-to.

Butch had sobered now, but showed no fear. "You don't seem to get the drift here, stranger. That's my kid brother Romer you just sucker punched. And us Sloan boys don't take no sass but sassparilla. Maybe if you light a shuck outta here right now, you'll see another sunrise."

Before Fargo could reply, a friendly but authoritative voice called out from the doorway: "All right, you two, let's break this up. You're ruining all the fun."

Fargo watched the man he assumed was Sheriff Cody Jeffries stroll into the saloon. He was a straw-haired man with a big, blunt, friendly face, thickset and strong-jawed with a bull neck. To Fargo he looked mighty prosperous for a man living on a lawman's wages: a dark suit of worsted wool, hand-tooled boots, a belt with a solid silver buckle and ivory inlay.

"Here now, Butch," the peace officer said, watching Romer slowly sit up, "what's all this ruckus about?"

Fargo leathered his Colt but kept his hand high on his right thigh.

"Cody," Butch said, "me, Romer, and Scout just come in to exercise our livers. I tipped my hat to Jessie and—whoa, mule!—this sorry son of a bitch pulled on us. He pistol-whipped Romer, and if you hadn't a come in, he'd a burned us down in cold blood."

Jessie bristled. "That's bunkum! Butch had no call to draw on this feller, Sheriff. It ain't fitten to paw on a girl like Butch done, nor to hit a woman like he done me, and this gent told him so."

"She's a damn liar," Butch protested. "I only went for my shooter after this lanky stranger drew his and coldcocked Romer."

The sheriff made a placatory gesture with his hands. "Now, boys, come down off your hind legs. No need to get your bowels in an uproar. This gent don't strike me as a cold-blooded killer. More likely he was forced to clear leather by your drunken shenanigans. Scout, what did you see?"

The skinny, furtive man at the table poured himself a shot. "You know me, Cody. I never see nothing."

Sheriff Jeffries turned his attention to Fargo. "How 'bout you, Mr.—?"

"Fargo."

"Mr. Fargo. Got anything to add to all this?"

Fargo considered it wise to take the easy way out. "You know how it is, Sheriff, when fellows get all jollified from whiskey."

Jeffries folded his arms over his massive chest. He glanced from Fargo to the two brothers. "Boys, such goings-on got no place in a civilized town. All right, so you had a bit of a frolic, but it's all over. From now on, watch those tempers."

Butch and Romer looked daggers at Fargo before they and Scout left the saloon.

"Mr. Fargo," Jeffries said, "I believe you acted in self-defense, so the law's got no mix in it. But the thing of it is, I'm trying to keep this town safe for everyone. All I ask is that you unlimber *only* as a last resort. Or to slice it another way: try to avoid letting things get out of hand. Most shootouts start as pissing contests—excuse my French, Jessie."

"That's a fair request, Sheriff," Fargo said. "I'll do my level best."

"'Preciate it." The sheriff extended his hand and Fargo shook it.

"If you don't mind my saying it," Fargo added, "you rule with a velvet fist, and it seems to work."

The sheriff shrugged one beefy shoulder. "I got no deputy, and this town has more weapons than a hound has fleas. That means you bend with the breeze or you break."

Fargo nodded. "That's how I'd play it, too. But these Sloan brothers strike me as the kind to nurse a grudge."

"Them two make a lot of noise when they're shellacked, Mr. Fargo, and they lack for parlor manners. But mostly they're bluff and bluster."

Fargo wasn't so sure about that, but Jeffries knew them best. "What about that cousin of theirs?"

"Bill Langley? Everybody calls him Scout. He's a helluva tracker, but he's a lunger. Too sick from consumption to do any fighting."

The sheriff sauntered out, and the musicians struck up "Buffalo Gals." Fargo produced a dime and smiled at Jessie. "Honor of the next dance?"

"My pleasure, Mr. Fargo, and you can poke that dime back into your pocket. I'm beholden. Most of the fellas in here are harmless, but not one of 'em will stand up to the Sloan boys. I'm Jessie Ravenel, by the way."

"Pleased. I'm Skye Fargo."

"Laws! I can see why they call you Skye. A body has to crane her neck to look up at you."

The smile she gave him was restive, as if she harbored secret thoughts. They whirled around the floor, the girl light as a feather when Fargo picked her up for the spins. He especially liked the way her long lashes curved against her cheeks when she closed her eyes.

"You have a lot of trouble with those Sloan boys?" he asked her.

"Enough, especially when they drink heavy. Mostly they drink at the Stardust. One thing this job has learned me: *All* men are just tomcats on the prowl."

But after looking up to study Fargo's face for a few moments, she added in a friendlier tone, "'Course, that's just nature's way. And some tomcats are more pleasin' than others."

Reluctantly, Fargo put his amorous thoughts aside and remembered his mission to gather information. "The sheriff seems like a decent sort," he remarked.

"Not too bad for a tin star," Jessie agreed in a wary tone.

This being Arkansas, Fargo wasn't sure if that tone was directed at Cody Jeffries personally or simply reflected the widespread mistrust in this region for any government authority.

"Mighty high-toned duds for an honest badge-toter," he remarked casually. "He looks more like a New York land hunter."

"He can afford to be honest. I hear his family's got money. His old man sells beef to the army."

Fargo nodded. "I guess the job attracts all types."

"I reckon," Jessie said. "The sheriff sugarcoated one thing, though."

"That being . . . ?"

"Scout Langley. That business about him being consumptive is true, and they say he can track an ant across bare stone. But he never blusters like his cousins—he just kills in the blink of an eye, never no warning. You watch him, Skye."

"I will, Jessie, thanks. But I'm just in town for a loafing spell."

She gave him an enigmatic smile. "You think I don't know that Skye Fargo is the Trailsman?"

"Hell, that's just claptrap drummed up by the ink-slingers to sell their crap sheets."

"If you say so."

Fargo thought it wise to change the subject. "You live here in town?"

"Mm-hm. I share a room at the hotel with Pattie, another of the dance girls. She's that tall redhead dancing with the fat fella. My folks got a farm three miles outside of town, but the drought has near ruint it. The sorghum didn't even come up last year, and I don't figure it aims to this year. The few cows we got left are all sick and giving thin milk with blood in it."

"Sorry to hear it. So you had to take this job?"

She nodded, her eyes filming. "Times is hard, Skye. Besides Ma and Pa, I got three brothers and a little sister. Most folks hereabouts is out of work. Ma says it's a long lane that has no turning, but if it don't turn quick, there's plenty will be starving."

A polite man in a bowler hat tapped Fargo's shoulder. "With your permission, sir, I'd like to purchase the next dance."

Fargo tipped his hat to Jessie and pressed an Indian head gold dollar into her hand. She looked flustered. "Skye, I hope you don't think I—"

"I think no such thing. Dancing with a girl as pretty as you is worth ten times this much. Enjoy your dance, friend," he said, handing her over to the new arrival.

But as Fargo walked off the dance floor, he thought about Jessie's report on the dire straits her family was in—and about Colonel Mackenzie's suspicion of the Ravenel males.

4

Fargo waited until the barkeep had an idle moment, then said, "Friend, I hear there's a few rooms for rent upstairs."

The saloon keeper grinned. "Damn straight I got a room for *you*. Mister, you got more guts than a smokehouse—I seen you handle the Sloan boys. You got a punch like a mule kick. Stay as long as you'd like. The best one's at the end of the hall with a window overlooking the street. C'mon, I'll show it you. Yo, Stacy!"

A grizzled old duffer playing dominoes at a front table limped up to the bar.

"Sling drinks until I get back," the barkeep told him. "Pour yourself a shot, but just one."

He led the way to a staircase at the back of the saloon.

"You realize, of course," the barkeep said as they ascended the bare wooden steps, "it gets a mite . . . busy up here, with the girls and all."

Even as the barkeep fell silent, Fargo heard a whore yell out, "Oh, *God*, you're the best, Jimmy!"

Fargo chuckled. "They're always the best when they're paying for it."

"No truer words, friend. I got a wife, and all she ever yells out is, 'Get your damn elbows off my hair!' "

Fargo followed him down a long, narrow hallway lined with doors and tin bracket candle sconces. Three men waited in the hallway, clutching whorehouse tokens purchased downstairs. The frontier was a masculine place, and a man searching for a wife had to marry anything that got off the train. But in the first-tier western states like Arkansas, sporting girls were in good supply.

The barkeep fished a skeleton key from his pocket and unlocked the last door on the right. The last of the day's light poured through the single sash window and revealed a small, bare, but reasonably clean room. An old stove with nickel trimmings sat on bricks in the middle of the room, and an iron bedstead covered with a shuck mattress stood in bowls of kerosene to keep off the bedbugs. A spur-scarred ladder-back chair and a wooden washstand with an enamel bowl, a pitcher, and a covered crockery jar for night soil completed the furnishings.

"There's a jakes out back, too," the barkeep said. "But pinch your nose—we got no honey wagon since Moss Harper died of brain fever. Nobody's lining up for the job."

There was no lamp in the room, but Fargo saw lead candle sconces, shaped like naked women, on the north and south walls.

"I'm thinking," the barkeep said, as if plucking the thought from Fargo's head, "that you'll want the bare window covered. I'll have one of the girls dig up a thick curtain."

"I'm obliged," Fargo said. He also appreciated the floor of foot-wide, unsanded boards with huge cracks between them. It allowed him a good view of the saloon below.

On their way back downstairs, one of the doors stood open, and a voluptuous blonde wearing only a red satin robe, untied, stood hip-cocked in the doorway, flashing Fargo a come-hither smile. In the fashion preferred by soiled doves, her eyebrows had been savagely plucked to form provocative curves.

"C'mon in, long-tall," she invited in a voice like honey poured over grits. "I'm free at the moment, and in your case I do mean *free.*"

Fargo had once taken the painful mercury cure for the dripping disease, and he had no plans to take it again—a distinct possibility when consorting with women who strapped on thirty to forty men a night.

"Thanks for the offer, sweet love, but my religion forbids it."

"Religion? *You*? That six-gun—that knife poking out of your boot—are they part of your devotions?"

Fargo winked at the barkeep and assumed a pious mien. "The Good Book commands us to smash the teeth of sinners."

"You done a good job of that downstairs. Dave, tell this handsome—"

"Put it out of your mind, Lynette. A whore who gives it away is no use to me."

"Yeah? Then maybe *you* better start paying for all the free rides, too. Or should I send the bill to your wife?"

"Your mouth runs like a whip-poor-will's ass," Dave shot back, tugging Fargo toward the stairs.

"Well, you want the room?" Dave asked when he was behind the bar. "I admit the price is dear—five bucks a week. Six will get you a room at the hotel and that includes hot baths."

Fargo produced a gold cartwheel and planked his cash. "It's steep," he agreed, "but prices soar when a town is booming."

"We got something you won't see much of at the hotel," Dave said, handing Fargo the key. "Felicity Meadows."

"She works here?" Fargo said in a surprised tone.

"What, you mean upstairs?" Dave laughed. "That'll be the day. No, she sings here four nights a week, and brother, that songbird don't come cheap. But she packs the house every show."

"Yeah, I can b'lieve that."

Through a front window Fargo watched a buckboard rattle to a stop. The slouch-hatted man driving it, who bore a striking resemblance to Jessie Ravenel, tied the reins to the brake and swung down, entering the saloon.

"Jake Ravenel," Dave explained. "Jessie's kid brother. There's two older brothers, too, and they're all wild cards."

"How wild?"

"They've busted this place up a few times, though they made the repairs themselves. And once they got into a shootout with soldiers from Fort Bowman. Nobody was killed, but one soldier got tagged in the hip."

Fargo studied Jake as his sister finished her dance. His corduroy pants had gone through at the knees, and his boots were held together with burlap strips. Despite a large frame he was clearly underweight. His trouble-seeking eyes and low-slung six-gun supported Colonel Mackenzie's surmise about the Ravenels, but if they were heisting payroll money, they sure weren't spending much on food or clothing.

Jessie tugged her brother toward the bar. "Skye, this here's my brother Jake. He come to town to sell a few pelts, and he stopped by to check on me."

Fargo offered his hand, and after a brief hesitation Jake shook it. His face was handsome in outline but raw from soap, sun, and wind.

"Sis told me what you done for her," Jake said. "I appreciate the hell right out of that. But Jess can be a mite too grateful sometimes, and it would be a big mistake if you took advantage of that. One look at you tells me you're the kind gets his way with the gals."

Despite Jake's clear message Fargo didn't feel he was being threatened—just warned by a protective brother. But the lad had a quick, nervous manner that put Fargo on guard. Such men could be hair-trigger.

"Don't worry, Jake. All I wanted from your sister was a dance," Fargo assured him.

"The day's a-comin'," Jake added, his voice strident with anger, "when me and my brothers will send them Sloan bastards and their back-shooting cousin up the flume."

"It's best to rile cool," Fargo advised.

"I'm hanged iffen I'll keep a cool head when the sons of bitches are fixen to"—he glanced at Jessie—"outrage my sis and kill my kin."

Fargo saw the dangerous, hot temper Colonel Mackenzie had mentioned about the Ravenel brothers. But hot-jawing was common on the frontier.

"It's none of my picnic," Fargo admitted. "But don't let your feelings run your brains."

"That's prob'ly good advice, Mr. Fargo," Jake said just before he left. "And you look like a fellow what would know. But I'm priddy near the end of my tether."

Jessie lingered a moment after her brother left. "Did you mean it when you told Jake *all* you wanted from me was a dance?"

Fargo grinned. "Sweetheart, he's your brother. Naturally I lied my tail off."

A smile lit up her pretty face. "That's all I wanted to know."

She returned to the busy dance floor and Fargo left the Razorback, boot heels thumping on the boardwalk as he bore toward the livery at the edge of town. The pink-and-gold clouds of sunset glowed on the western horizon, and a boy of twelve or thirteen was busy lighting lamps hung on iron poles.

Fargo was crossing an alley between the Half Moon Café and the Overland Stage and Freighting office when a heated voice, well back in the alley, caught his attention. There was just

35

enough light for Fargo to make out Sheriff Cody Jeffries and the Sloan brothers, Butch and Romer.

Fargo couldn't make out the words, but Jeffries appeared to be reading them the riot act while the other two listened submissively. This was a side of himself the sheriff hadn't displayed in the saloon. Maybe, Fargo thought, this was the way Jeffries chose to operate: calm and amiable in public, implacable in private. If so, it wasn't a bad approach.

Fargo had just cleared the alley when a youthful voice cried out, "Jesus Christ! *Duck*, mister!"

Years of frontier survival had conditioned Fargo's body to react from pure reflex without waiting for commands from his mind. The same instant he heard the voice he didn't just duck, he fell in a flat sprawl onto the boardwalk even as a sharp *thwack* punctuated the sounds of Main Street.

Fargo rolled instantly and quickly off the boardwalk and into the street. As he rose to his knees he jerked back his short iron and thumb-cocked it. Just to his right, a throwing knife deeply embedded in a support beam still quivered slightly from the force of the throw. Had Fargo not moved in time, it would be buried in his back.

But watching the boardwalk behind him, Fargo spotted no one suspicious looking. An elderly couple emerging from the mercantile store, a drunk practically walking on his knees, and the young lamplighter, who now raced toward Fargo.

"Cripes! You all right, mister?"

Fargo pushed to his feet. "Sure, kid, thanks to you. Didja see who tossed it?"

"No, sir, not to describe him. The light's weak on this side of the street. I guess he was hiding in one of the doorways. I saw somebody step out real quick like, and I seen the knife when his arm went back."

"You see which way he ran off?"

"To the other side of the street. A freight wagon was rolling past, and the dust hid him. When the wagon cleared, he was gone."

Fargo noticed the sheriff hadn't come out of the alley to investigate, but he might not have heard the kid shout. With an effort he yanked the knife out of the beam. It was a lethal but

cheap throwing knife of a type sold all over out west for six bits—
any of a hundred men in Pine Hollow could have thrown it.

"What's your name, son?"

"Jimmy Parker, sir."

"Well, Jimmy Parker is a name I'm going to remember for
the rest of my life—a life I owe to you. Stick this in your pocket."

Jimmy goggled at the five-dollar quarter eagle Fargo pressed
into his hand. "Holy moly! I'm rich! *Thanks*, mister!"

Fargo shook the young hero's hand and resumed his walk
toward the livery, much more vigilant. It was grainy twilight
now, and several lamps burned in the big livery barn. Fargo saw
that Dolomite had turned the Ovaro out into the paddock instead
of stalling him, just as Fargo had requested.

He went into the tack room and unbuckled one of his saddlebags.

"That you, Fargo?" Cranky Man's voice called from the hayloft.

"It's me. Relax."

Carrying the saddlebag, Fargo climbed the wooden rungs up
into the loft. Soft lamplight showed Cranky Man resting on his
rainproof Navajo blanket spread over the hay.

"This beats my corn shuck mattress all to hell," Fargo
greeted him.

"Best bed I've had in many moons," Cranky Man agreed.
"How'd it go?"

Fargo told him about his near-deadly encounter with the
Sloan brothers, about meeting Jessie and Jake Ravenel, the sheriff, and the attempt on his life.

"Who you think tossed the knife?" Cranky Man asked.

"Too soon to say. But if I had to wager, I'd put my money on
Scout Langley. He looks like the type who knows how to cover
and conceal. Besides, he wasn't in the alley when Jeffries was
chewing out the Sloan boys."

"Two attempts to kill you on your first day in town," Cranky
Man mused. "This place is bad medicine. I say we pull foot."

Fargo snorted. "You're going puny on me already? If you
ain't got the caliber for the job, roll your blanket and raise dust."

"Ah, cowplop. Am I getting paid?"

"You ever known me to be a piker? We'll go snooks on
whatever I make. Stick or quit?"

"That's fair. I'll stick. A man can only die once."

"In that case . . ."

Fargo pulled an old but well-maintained Colt's Dragoon from the saddlebag. "You might need this. That New Haven rifle of yours is a good weapon, but the barrel's too long for close-in work."

"You know I can't hit a bull in the butt with a short gun. 'Sides, that old relic is cap and ball, I can't—"

"It *was* cap and ball. I had it rechambered to take factory ammo. This little honey will stop a stagecoach. But brace yourself if you fire it—it's got a kick like a Missouri mule."

"Might be handy, at that," Cranky Man agreed, taking the big weapon.

"But don't cart it around town openly," Fargo cautioned. "An Indian going around heeled in Pine Hollow will hit the ground before his shadow can move."

"All right. What's the sheriff like?"

"It's a mite queer," Fargo replied. "The sheriff's friendly, but the town isn't. And it's not because Jeffries is a sissy-boy—he's one of the toughest starmen I've seen."

"Them Ravenels you mentioned," Cranky Man said. "I was jawing with Dolomite, and he gave me some lowdown on that clan. They sell him moonshine at a fair price, but he said the three boys was *contrabandistas* down in Mexico until they was chased out by the Federals."

"Running guns?"

Cranky Man shook his head. "Sounded like penny-ante truck to me. Tequila, clothing, and such."

"That's just joker poker," Fargo agreed. "Lots of that going on. Doesn't make them genuine owlhoots. Then again, it doesn't make them scrubbed angels, either. Colonel Mackenzie could be right about them. But these Sloan brothers and their skinny ferret of a cousin bear watching, too. They definitely got the outlaw stink on them."

"You sleeping in the livery?" Cranky Man asked.

"Nah. I took a room above the Razorback Saloon."

"Fargo, you damn hypocrite. You told me once that soft beds make soft soldiers."

"*This* soft bed is smack in the middle of a cathouse."

Cranky Man flashed his mirthless grin. "That's different. You're not a soldier anyhow."

He removed the wrinkled sack of horehound candy from his shirt. "Horehound for a whore hound?"

Fargo grinned as he selected a piece. "You crack a good one now and then, you worthless redskin. How 'bout I stand you to a good meal?"

"A meal for an Injin? Where—a pig trough?"

"You're a breed, not pure quill. The Half Moon Café is open late. Let's put a feed bag on."

Inky fathoms of darkness cloaked this far end of town, offering both safety and danger to anyone on the street. Fargo and Cranky Man moved down the middle of the wide street, which remained dark even when they reached the lamp-lit section.

"Hold on," Fargo said, glancing toward the boarded-up dance hall. Pine Hollow had no newspaper yet, but broadsheets were plastered up when there was news. The yellow glow of a lamp showed one on the front of the dance hall. Fargo crossed the street.

Out loud, he read about the latest robbery.

"How's come," Cranky Man said when he finished, "it says three men done it? I counted five."

"Same here. That's a mite curious, innit?"

"So happens," Cranky Man said, "there's three of these Ravenel boys. Maybe it's a . . . whatchacallit."

"Frame-up? Could be. But there were soldiers who witnessed the heist and got away. Might be the ink-slinger just got it wrong—today's headlines wrap tomorrow's garbage. Besides, the Sloan brothers and their cousin make three, too."

The Half Moon Café was well lighted but nearly deserted. A small sign over the entrance bragged WE'RE A BROKEN DRUM—CAN'T BE BEAT!!! The two new arrivals were only a few feet inside the building when a potbellied, balding man with purple bags like bruises under his eyes called out from behind the counter:

"That red son ain't welcome here. This café is for white folks only. No coloreds, no Mexers, no Injuns."

"Hell, brother, I ain't Indian," Cranky Man retorted before Fargo could stop him. "My people came over on the *Mayflower*."

"Serve it on toast."

"I'd ruther biscuits."

"Dust, John."

Fargo stepped on the Choctaw's foot to silence him. "I respect your policy," Fargo said politely. "But this man's father was a soldier killed in the service of his country. It's true his mother is a Choctaw, but Soaring Eagle here is a U.S. Army scout. He's led soldier blue to dozens of renegade camps and helped clear this area for settlement."

Only the part about Cranky Man's father and mother was true, but Fargo sounded convincing. The man pulled at the point of his chin, debating.

"Well, mister," he said to Fargo, "that breed don't look so consequential to me. But you sure do, and I'm damned if I'm fool enough to call you a liar. All right, I'll feed him on account he's with you. But no hard-times tokens—I want cash money, over the counter."

A drummer wearing a straw boater, his sample case on a chair beside him, was the only other customer in the café. Fargo and Cranky Man scraped back two chairs at a table in the center of the room. Fargo kept a close eye on the door, that knife attack from earlier still fresh in his mind.

"Soaring Eagle?" Cranky Man whispered to Fargo. "Christ Almighty, should I do a rain dance?"

"All I got left," the plump proprietor called out to them, "is beef and biscuits or corn pone and back ribs."

Fargo ordered the ribs, Cranky Man the beef.

"Listen," Fargo said, keeping his voice low, "you keep giving the rough side of your tongue to these locals and you're gonna get your tail in a crack."

"You don't mind my talk."

"Any man who saves my life can insult me six ways till Sunday. But these are strangers who got no use for Indians, especially with dozens of tribes right next door that could strike the warpath at any minute. Just sew up your lips around them."

"I'll try, but they don't call me Cranky Man for nothing."

The drummer, who had one of those faces forgotten the moment it was seen, called over to Fargo, "You aim to roost here, sir?"

"No, friend, just a short visit."

"Well, I'm from Jonesboro myself, but you could do worse than Pine Hollow, for a surety you could. This town is going great guns. Oh, they need more boardwalks for the ladies, and they got no fast-mail riders—just jackass mail. But soon Pine Hollow will be a going concern."

Fargo agreed, which was exactly why he would light a shuck for the wilderness when his job was done. He had been fleeing from "cussed syphillization" most of his life, preferring the high lonesome and pristine valleys over a gaggle of dough bellies who couldn't even feed or clothe themselves without stores.

"I'll keep that in mind," he replied politely, adding truthfully, "mighty pretty country hereabouts."

The proprietor came over with two steaming platters and set them down. "Name's Tubby Blackford, gents. Actually, the front name is Roy, but folks call me Tubby on account I eat too much of my own cooking."

He looked at Cranky Man. "Soaring Eagle, this longhorn beef I get from southeast Texas is so damn tough I got to beat it with a cleaver before I cook it. Elsewise, it'll bust your teeth."

"You cooked it?" Cranky Man retorted, unable to cut it. "I thought it was jerky."

Fargo winced as Blackford's face hardened. "You don't like my cooking, blanket ass, go back to the rez and eat maggoty pork and hardtack."

"And why don't you—"

"Pack it in, Soaring Eagle," Fargo muttered, cutting Cranky Man off. Looking at Blackford, he said, "It's fine cooking, Tubby, best ribs I ever tasted."

"That's what these three soldiers told me today. They—"

All of an instant Blackford fell silent, staring at Fargo. Immediately Fargo knew why—those soldiers had spread the rumor about a bearded, buckskin-clad man being among the holdup gang. Tubby went back behind the counter and began to knead biscuit dough, casting furtive glances at Fargo.

"We best work fast," Fargo said between mouthfuls, "or vigilantes are going to fit us for hemp neckties."

"Don't look now," Cranky Man muttered, "but here comes the town booster."

Uninvited, the drummer joined them at their table, trailing a reek of whiskey.

"You gents need to glom my wares," he said, opening his sample case. It was packed with combs, brushes, hair ribbons, and sewing notions.

"A bunch of damned flub dubs," Cranky Man said.

But Fargo plucked out a metal tube filled with phosphors. "Usually I'm not much for progress, but these beat the hell right out of flint and steel."

"No truer words, friend, no truer words. That'll be four bits."

The price was steep, but Fargo paid it just to get rid of the pest. The two men finished eating, squared the bill, and went back out into the dark street.

"You best hightail it back to the livery," Fargo told his friend. "And keep that Dragoon close by. I'm going back to the saloon and see what I can nose up."

"Gonna get your bell rope pulled, too, uh?"

"A man can always hope, but I doubt it. This is work, not pleasure."

"As I recall, you always find time to mix the two."

But as Fargo angled across the street toward the Razorback, he recalled how a kid's shouted warning had narrowly saved him from death. And experience taught him there might not be a warning next time.

5

Even before Fargo parted the batwings, he could tell the Razor-back was in a rollicking tumult. Shouts, laughter, and lively music greeted his ears, and the pungent odor of tobacco leaked out into the street. He pushed quietly inside, exciting little notice, and surveyed the crowded saloon.

Almost immediately he noticed the dangerous trio of Butch and Romer Sloan and their weasel of a cousin Scout, seated at a table beside the dance floor. But all three were studiously ignoring Fargo even though they saw him watching them, a fact that instantly put him on his guard.

The dime-a-dance girls, Jessie included, were all out on the dance floor, with a line of men waiting their turns. At the bar, a middle-aged dandy with silver muttonchops and a melting chin was pontificating to a group of men, apparently keeping his audience listening by supplying them with drinks.

Fargo moved to the edge of the group at the bar and ordered a shot of rye from Dave the barkeep, cocking one ear toward the blowhard.

"Gentlemen, it is a common mistake to confuse the term *corpus delicti* with corpse. *Corpus delicti* refers to all the material evidence in a homicide, and indeed, establishes whether a murder has even been committed, whereas . . ."

Fargo snorted, taking in the speaker's white duck trousers, frilled shirt, satin vest, and flamboyant scarlet coat with gold buttons. He had met this nickel-chasing type often out west. On the frontier, where most men couldn't even read, any man who had peeked into a law book could set himself up as a Philadelphia lawyer.

"Boys," he rambled on, "naturally these recent holdups are

heinous crimes, and the perpetrators must be brought to justice. Law and order must triumph, and it's a good thing when a town like this settles up—to a point. But allow too many women and churches, and the next thing you know the mealymouthed psalm-singers and militant temperance biddies will be calling the shots."

"Yeah, McGrady!" a voice farther back in the saloon called out. "And that puts jackleg lawyers like you out of business!"

"Jackleg? Sir, you're flirting with slander. I'll have you know that I've argued three hundred cases before the bar in Balti-more."

"You mean *in* the bar, you drunken sot!"

Laughter rippled through the saloon, and Fargo moved quietly on, carrying out his orders from Colonel Mackenzie: eavesdrop-ping, observing, and—as Fargo viewed it—spending as much gov-ernment money as possible.

"Skye!"

Jessie's melodic voice arrested his attention and drew him to the dance floor.

"How's come you're not dancing with me?" she pouted, whirl-ing him around as the duet struck up "Turkey in the Straw." "A body could feel neglected."

"I'd never neglect your body," he assured her.

Jessie punched his arm but smiled at the pun. "Don't mock the way I talk. You know what I mean."

"Well, looks to me like there's quite a few jaspers ahead of me in line, pretty lady. And if looks could kill, right now I'd be dead six times over."

"Oh, poof, they can go to blazes. Some are nice fellas—just lonely. But a smart chance of these local chawbacons figure a dime buys 'em more than a dance—like a feel or two."

"Just send them upstairs," Fargo suggested.

"You mean where you live now?" Jessie grinned impishly. "You best watch that tart Lynette—she'll give you some free, all right, but hide your money pouch."

"I'd be wiser," Fargo replied, "to forget Lynette and watch those three at the edge of the dance floor. You noticed they're back?"

"Of course. And they're behaving theirselves—that makes a body nervous. Them sneaky polecats are planning somethin'."

"Who's that nabob at the bar?" Fargo asked. "The one dressed like a medicine-show barker and spouting law?"

"J. C. McGrady. He's what they call a remittance man—paid by his rich family to go west and get out of their hair. Now he's set up as a lawyer. He claims as how he apprenticed with a law office in Baltimore, but I think he makes up most of his legal bosh."

"You figure him for a serious criminal?"

"He's just a pain in the sitter. Always trying to sue everybody. Skye?"

"Hmm?"

"How's come you ask so many questions about everybody? Are you private police?"

Fargo laughed, gazing down into her pretty, sea-green eyes. "The hell brought that on?"

"Most men holding me in their arms ask about me."

"I don't wonder. All right, here's one I been curious about—it's plain you hate this job, so why take it?"

"Like I already told you, us Ravenels are just hoe-men. Pa says we're paperwork rich but pocket poor. He owns six hundred acres in a land grant for service in the Indian wars. But two years in a row now, grasshoppers and drought have ruint our crops. I have to help the family."

Fargo had indeed already asked her the same question earlier that day. And both times her answer seemed sincere. If the Ravenel boys, as Colonel Mackenzie and Sheriff Jeffries had hinted, were pulling off payroll and supply heists, why would they let their attractive sister literally fall into the hands of horny men in a saloon? Then again, Fargo thought, it was a perfect cover while they stashed away their cut of the swag. After all, why did she make that "private police" remark?

"Skye?"

"Yeah?"

"It's a mite odd, don'tcha think, you showing up here outta the blue?"

"Are we back to the private police theory?"

"No, I believe you—I guess. But I wish you *was* the law. See . . . there's talk."

Fargo spun her around, feeling her small, tight waist fit perfectly in his hands. "This is about me being part of a holdup gang, huh?"

"Uh-hunh. That's the talk."

"It's air pudding, that's all. And I'm not the only one being accused."

"Maybe not. You're the mysterious stranger in town. Take a glance around."

Fargo did. He caught many men looking at him, but their eyes slid away quickly from his. Yet, the Sloan brothers and Scout Langley were still purposely avoiding him. Fargo vowed again to watch them closely. That knife hadn't tossed itself.

"You know," Jessie said close to his ear, her breath moist, warm, and soft, "some even say you and my brothers are in it together. You believe that?"

"Tote up the number of fools in any town," Fargo said, "and you'll have a clear enough majority."

The dance ended and Fargo reluctantly yielded Jessie to a doltish-looking man in a wrinkled sack suit. He bought another whiskey, then drifted back to join a ring of men at the rear of the saloon. He watched a sharper in a brocade vest fleece several men at a green-baize card table, dealing from the bottom of the deck while distracting his victims with witty patter.

The sharper raised his eyes to meet Fargo's. "Care to test your pasteboard abilities, sport? I'll keep it simple for a rustic like you."

"No, thanks. You appear to be on a roll, and I barely know the game."

The sharper gave him a wire-tight smile, knowing otherwise. "Maybe some other time, sport. You look like a fast learner."

"Maybe so."

The music suddenly stopped and a multicolored spotlight—comprised of a huge railroad lantern with a man moving several bottles of colored liquid in front of it—glowed to life. A thunderous cheer rose as Felicity Meadows appeared as if by magic on a stage along the south wall of the saloon.

Fargo was transfixed. She looked storybook perfect in a pinch-waisted, royal blue, silk and lace gown and wearing sheer white gloves to her elbows. Her wheat-blond hair was tightly back-combed and held in place with a silver tiara. Kohl had been artfully applied to lengthen her eyebrows and shade the lids. The effect was to make a stunningly beautiful woman even more exotic and unattainable.

"Good god-*damn*," said a man standing next to Fargo, "don't *she* fire up your boiler? A swing like that belongs on the porch."

"Boys," another man said, "I'd give a purty to strip that gal buck."

"See *Fel* naked? Brother, you're more likely to catch a weasel asleep."

Fargo edged closer to the stage as Felicity began singing a sweet, mesmerizing rendition of "My Old Kentucky Home." With her regal manner and luxurious wardrobe, as well as a golden-toned singing voice, she tamed every man in the audience into a stunned silence. Unlike the lowly soiled doves or the semirespectable dime-a-dance girls, she reined over the Razorback with the languid hauteur of a Parisian diva.

Next she sang "Listen to the Mockingbird," then finished her brief act with a French song that brought the house down, "La Belle Dame Sans Merci." For this last number she pulled out a graceful little fan with gold sequins, playing peekaboo with her audience. As she sang she flowed smooth as liquid across the stage, hips swaying in an easy, gliding rhythm that held every man in stunned admiration.

Several times Felicity's eyes met Fargo's directly, but only to scorn him by her look—just as she had done the first time she laid eyes on him at the livery. He didn't realize Jessie was by his side until she whispered in his ear, "You musta peed her off, Skye. Didja try to speak to her without requesting permission?"

In the midst of an explosion of applause, Felicity left by a door behind the stage.

"First dibs," Fargo told Jessie, pressing a dime into her hand as the musicians resumed the dance music.

"I reckon you figure Fel's the top of the heap?" Jessie asked him as they danced. "All the rest do."

"A woman as fetching as you," Fargo replied, "has no call to be jealous."

"That's the truth. She ain't worth being jealous over."

"Sounds like you're not too fond of her?"

"It's nothing to do with me. She's too fine-haired for the rest of us—all silky satin. Won't even look us in the eyes."

"She's stuck on herself, for a fact," Fargo agreed. "And speak-

47

ing of silky satin—can she possibly make enough money singing in this watering hole to afford clothes like that?"

Jessie looked up into his face and flashed a wicked grin. "You ain't the first to wonder, Skye. She's got a smart chance more of them gowns and dresses."

"Curious," Fargo said.

"It gets more curiouser. She's also got the best room at the hotel—half the top floor. Three times the reg'lar room rate. And keeps her a horse at the livery. Seems a mite queer, don't it?"

"All right, I'll bite. Who's keeping her?"

Jessie shook her head. "That's her little secret. Some say it's Dave, but that's hogwash. He ain't got the kinda money Her Majesty requires, and he couldn't hide it from his nosy wife. Anyhow, I reckon that's what the horse is for—to go meet whoever it is."

Fargo mulled all this even as he kept an eye on the unholy trio at the table. They were neither watching him nor bothering the dance girls—just drinking themselves into a flush-faced drunk. Some purpose lay behind their grim determination, and Fargo planned to be ready for it.

Jessie's voice broke into his thoughts. "Holding me kinda tight, ain'tcha, Skye?"

"Is that a complaint?"

"No, just wondering why."

"Faint heart never won fair lady."

"Am I as fair as Her Nibs?"

"There you go again. How does a man compare two beautiful roses?"

"*This* one's kissed the Blarney Stone," she replied, adding, "but I like it."

An impatient customer tapped Fargo on the shoulder, and he surrendered Jessie to her next paying partner. For the next hour or so he nursed a couple more shots at the bar and listened in on the conversations around him. Dave remained friendly, and no one accosted Fargo, but no one sat next to him either—the rumor, Fargo surmised, could soon grow into a dangerous certainty if he didn't work fast.

Arkansas's strictly enforced "grog shop" law required all establishments serving liquor to close by midnight. At twenty till Dave sounded last call, and Fargo slipped upstairs. The sporting girls had serviced their last clients, and all the doors were closed. Fargo made it to his room unobserved and let himself in, Colt at the ready.

Fargo lit one of the candles. Skeleton keys were widely available, and the weak hook-and-eye lock on the inside of the door could be forced by a child. Fargo tied his belt to the door latch and secured the other end to a leg of the stove. Not exactly tight security, but it would buy him a few precious seconds if someone forced the door.

He blew out the candle and sprawled on the floor, peering through the wide cracks between floorboards. Jessie and the other dance girls left, then the last customers—including the Sloan brothers and their cousin.

Dave locked up, blew out the wall lamps, and left for his house in town. But Fargo was acutely aware of the outside stairs, around back, that led up to his floor.

He moved the rickety ladder-back chair to the north wall of his room, out of the line of fire from the door, and waited, Colt in hand. He listened to the odd noises flimsy wooden buildings make after dark—the groaning and creaking of joists and support beams. There were also a few odd moans coming from the room of a soiled dove who had taken on an all-nighter. The sounds forced Fargo to shift in his chair as he recalled the perfect fit of Jessie's body to his.

More time dragged by, and the tall case clock in the hallway chimed the quarter hour—which quarter, or which hour, Fargo wasn't sure. His eyelids felt weighted with coins, and he began to think he'd guessed wrong—there was no game afoot tonight.

Then, the sound slapping him awake like cold water, a floorboard creaked outside his door.

A few seconds later, the door latch rattled quietly.

Here's the fandango, Fargo thought, thumb-cocking his six-gun.

The latch rattled a bit harder, and Fargo slid his finger inside the trigger guard and curled it around the trigger. His belt was some protection, but one sharp tug on that door would likely bust the latch, and he planned to get the first shot off.

"Skye?" called a low, soft female voice he recognized. "Are you asleep?"

"Jessie? For Christ sakes, lady! Are you alone?"

"No. I brought witnesses to see me shamelessly come to a man's room. Do you want me to go or stay?"

"Hang on, hon."

Fargo leathered his Colt, untied the belt, and unlocked the door, opening it. Jessie, her long hair loose and flowing over her shoulders, ducked quickly inside.

"Girl, you been grazing locoweed? You damn near got plugged."

Fargo secured the door again and lit one of the candles.

"You mad at me for coming? You want me to go?"

"I never said that. But you know damn well I got enemies in this town."

"Well, we can't meet in my hotel room on account I share it. So as soon as Pattie fell asleep, I slipped out."

A smile lifted one corner of Fargo's mouth. "I thought you were a good girl who only gives a man a dance?"

"I am, but this is one night I forgot to wear my halo."

She stepped up on tiptoes and gave Fargo a deep, probing kiss that set his heart racing and instantly stiffened his manhood. The volcanic pressure in his groin pressed for release.

"Usually," she said when she pulled back slightly, "I just see how close I can get to the fire without being burned. But the moment I met you, I wanted all the heat I could get."

Earlier Fargo had enjoyed dancing with this pretty, alluring girl. But holding her close, feeling her perfect female form meld to his body and her silky hair tickling his cheeks, he wondered how she might be at the best dance of all, the mazy waltz—a dance of erotic delight he hadn't enjoyed in long weeks on the trail.

"If it's heat you want," Fargo said, unbuckling his gun belt, "you're going to get plenty. It's been a while for me."

Jessie started undoing the button loops of her dress. "It's been a spell for me, too. Longer than for you, I expect. I'm plagued most to death by men wantin' to do it, but I hardly never give in. With you, I wanted to right off. I couldn't help noticing when we danced close—you felt hard as sacked salt . . . *every* part of you."

Jessie shimmied out of her dress, leaving it in a puddle at her feet. Now only a chemise of thin muslin covered her, emphasizing the dark triangle of her bush and the two large impressions made by her nipples. Fargo tugged the chemise over her head and made her gasp with surprised pleasure when he took each spearmint-tasting nipple in turn into his mouth and sucked and nipped at them.

"Oh, Skye, you got me hotter than a branding iron already! Show me your hard peeder. Ever since I felt it, it's all I can think about."

Fargo opened his fly and his unleashed manhood sprang out into full view in the candlelight, making Jessie's eyes widen in astonishment. "Laws! Skye . . . my lands, you take my breath away! If that thing was any bigger it would live next door."

Effortlessly, Fargo picked her up and placed her on the bed. "Oh, I think you can make Mr. J. Henry feel at home right . . . here."

He parted her satin-smooth thighs, and his fingers showed her exactly the moist, chamois-soft home he meant.

"God yes," she moaned between keening, mewling sounds. *That's* his home. Send him in, please? Right now?"

Eager to oblige, heartbeat exploding in his ears like Pawnee war drums, Fargo rolled into the saddle and filled her love nest to the hilt with a fast thrust of his hips. Almost immediately Jessie's pent-up need exploded in her first of many climaxes, and they only grew in intensity as Fargo drove harder and faster, feeling his own volcano rush toward explosive release. In the final moments, fueled by each other's pyrotechnic passion, they achieved the ultimate peak as one in a shuddering, uncontrollable spasm that left them both barely conscious for uncounted minutes.

But for Fargo, pleasure always had to come in broken doses surrounded by danger. As soon as his mind and body functioned again as a team, he warned Jessie of the danger. She dressed, gave him a last, lingering kiss, and Fargo let her out. He still hadn't secured the belt when there was a light tap on the door and a feminine whisper: "Skye?"

Convinced it was Jessie, he opened the door to a slyly grinning Lynette. "Got anything left for me, long-tall?" she greeted him.

"For a gal who sells it all night, you sure seem eager to give it away."

"Oh, don't be an old sobersides. You'll like it."

Fargo glanced past her down the hallway. All seemed clear. "Never been a time when I didn't," he assured her.

"Why'n'cha let me in? That farm gal is pretty, but she don't know beans about jiggling a man's handle. I can work it all night and make you bark like a dog."

Fargo's eyes narrowed in speculation. "You *been* working it all night, Lynette. The longest line was outside your door. You know, a man doesn't meet too many sporting girls who fill their spare time by giving their favors away."

"And a sporting girl don't meet too many stallions like you."

Fargo wasn't vain enough to swallow that. "Could it be that you've been paid to keep a close eye on me—maybe even tire me out so killers can get the jump on me?"

"Balderdash! Do men require pay to keep a close eye on Fel? C'mon, strap me on and see if you can buck me off."

In fact, despite his tumble with Jessie, Lynette's steamy talk had Fargo hard as a poker. But his strong survival instinct warned him off. He had taken a big enough chance with Jessie. If Lynette was half as talented she boasted she was, he could be in the heat of the act, blissfully distracted, when a bullet snapped his spine.

"Sleep tight, m'love," Fargo told her. "You're a pretty gal and a powerful temptation, but I need my beauty sleep."

"Oh, all right," she pouted as he started to nudge the door shut. "But write this on your pillowcase: *Any*time you want it, you can point my heels to the sky. Toodle-oo, long-tall."

6

Fully dressed, his gun belt and knife on the floor beside the bed, Fargo stretched out on top of the blanket, but despite his weariness sleep eluded him at first. Jessie's honeysuckle perfume lingered in the bed, clashing oddly with his memory of the hateful looks Felicity had given him tonight. Just who was keeping that elegant and haughty woman in such fine style?

Through the room's only window, which Dave had forgotten to cover with a curtain, Fargo saw a vast sky peppered silver with stars. He wished he was sleeping out under them right now, no walls and ceiling caging him like an animal. Those worn-out beams and joists he'd noticed earlier creaked even louder as the wee hours approached, sounding like men creeping up on him.

At some point Fargo's eyes eased shut and his limbs went heavy in sleep. He had worried about only the door because this was the second story. With the abruptness of a thunderclap, he was rudely awakened by breaking glass, a hard thump on the floor, and the crackling hiss of a fuse.

With reflexive urgency Fargo fought down a welling of fear. He couldn't spot the explosive anywhere, and he knew he'd never get the well-secured door open in time. Fargo rolled off the bed and groped desperately under it. His fingers closed on a round metal can—blasting powder used by miners and the U.S. Army.

He couldn't feel the fuse, which meant it had already burned into the well and was only heartbeats away from detonating enough black powder to blow him into confetti. With no time to waste standing back up, he hurled it back through the broken window. But it had just barely cleared before the back-blast blew the entire window and frame out and rolled Fargo, ears ringing loudly, hard back into the wall behind him.

The concussion dulled his hearing, but he could hear some of the girls screaming. As the clamor rose, he shook his head a few times, then grabbed his weapons and fumbled the door open, dashing into the hallway. Several female heads peeked out from open doorways.

"No need to have a conniption fit, ladies. The trouble's over. Go on back to bed."

Fargo used the rear stairway, filling his hand with blue steel and searching the darkness carefully. The explosion could have been a diversionary ruse with killers waiting to cut him down as he investigated the blast. But he made it to the ground safely and hurried around to the street.

Using his newly purchased lucifers, Fargo struck several matches in a row as he searched the dirt under the window. Several different sets of boot prints confused the issue, but Fargo isolated the most recent by their strong edges that hadn't yet crumbled. Close examination revealed a ridge in the left print where a chunk of the heel had broken off.

Fargo heard someone approaching in the darkness. "Friend or foe?" he called out, cocking his gun. "If I don't recognize your voice, you best freeze."

"We ain't swapping spit, Fargo," Cranky Man's sarcastic voice replied, "but I guess I'm a friend."

Cranky Man drew up beside him, the Colt's Dragoon making a big lump behind his shirt.

"Still above the ground, uh?" he greeted Fargo.

"Yeah, with about a half second to spare. Christ, at first I thought this job was going to be money for old rope. Now I see I'm up against it."

No crowd was forming, and Fargo realized the powerful blast had left the locals afraid to leave their homes. That might help preserve any additional tracks.

"Any idea who did it?" Cranky Man asked.

"That's a poser, all right. Especially since I didn't hear any getaway hooves pounding afterward. It could be a lone wolf who's still hiding in the area. C'mon."

The two men searched the nearby doorways and alleys. Fargo even checked the flimsy wooden jakes behind the saloon.

"I'm thinking it was one of the Sloan boys or their cousin," Cranky Man conjectured. "Sounds like you gelded them pretty good yesterday. Or maybe it was that peckerwood you scared at the livery."

"Could be either one of them," Fargo agreed. "But chucking explosions is pretty extreme revenge for a man that's only lost a pissing contest. Looks to me like somebody either knows, or maybe has guessed, why I'm here. Happens that's so, this blast is just the beginning, old son."

Cranky Man grunted. "Most likely, that knife that almost killed you was the beginning. Just like I said—Fargo's in town just one day, and hell's a-poppin'."

"And like I said, get used to it because whoever these egg-sucking varmints are, they plan on dealing us misery. This is two attempts to kill me in one day. We best take it by the horns or it's a nameless grave for us."

"Taking it by the horns ain't what the colonel ordered you to do."

"It ain't his ass on the line, either," Fargo retorted. "I'll play it his way whenever I can, but he's behind a desk and we're out in the tall weeds."

"I still think we ought to put this burg behind us and go find a safe cave."

"Patience, my friend. The worm will turn. We just got to town. Besides, it's not my way to rabbit after some scum bucket tries to kill me."

Fargo caught a whiff of the Choctaw's breath. "You best spend less time with O B Joyful. They'll be coming after you, too."

A horse cantered into town from the west. "What's all the whoop-de-doo?" Sheriff Jeffries's voice called out. "I live two miles out of town, yet some damn blast woke me up."

While the sheriff dismounted from his buckskin gelding, Fargo muttered in Cranky Man's ear: "The place for a lawman to sleep is on a cot in the jailhouse."

Fargo noticed the sheriff's tooled, high-cantled saddle—top-quality work. But Jessie had mentioned that his family was rich, and besides, even poor men took pride in scrimping and saving for a top-notch saddle.

Fargo explained about the blasting powder but said nothing about the prints he'd found.

"Guess you jumped over a snake that time, Fargo," Jeffries

said, eyeing Cranky Man but saying nothing. "'Pears to me you've got a serious enemy, though for the life of me I can't see why. You're a polite, soft-spoken cuss. I ain't one to nose a man's back-trail, but is there maybe something you're holding back?"

"Don't forget, Sheriff, whoever *tossed* that powder is the criminal, not me."

"Hell, I know that. But, you see, a little bird flew in my window tonight and told me you . . . visited with Jessie Ravenel earlier."

"Does that break a law? She's not married."

"Of course not. The fornication laws were struck down years ago. And Jessie is a tempting little armful. But, you see, her three brothers are a mighty protective bunch. They once beat the dog shit out of some jasper just for stealing a kiss from her."

Fargo hadn't considered the Ravenel boys as culprits in the explosion, but did so now. Jake had indeed seemed protective of his sister. "If they're all that concerned, why would they let her dance in a saloon?"

"These are hard times, Mr. Fargo, and a pretty girl is an asset. Then again, maybe her working in the saloon is meant to make the family *look* poor."

Fargo had entertained the same thought. If the Ravenels were accumulating swag, putting their pretty sister to work might deflect suspicion.

"Either way," the sheriff added, "it's one thing to let her dance with men, another to let her make whoopee with them."

"That shines," Fargo agreed. "But the Ravenel boys sure found out quick, if it was them. And it ain't easy for poor dirt-scratchers to lay hands on U.S. Army blasting caps."

"Oh, those Ravenels just might be more than farmers, I'd wager. The boys, at least. And one of the heists recently was a weapons shipment to Fort Bowman."

"More than farmers?" Fargo repeated. "Is that according to Dame Rumor or the facts?"

"Little of both, I'd say. But I don't set much stock in rumors, Mr. Fargo, or I'd have to arrest you."

"For being a holdup man, right?"

Jeffries nodded. "So some say. Your description has been mentioned."

"You believe it?"

"My first impression tells me you're not the type. So does your reputation. Besides, the same fools who spread the rumors about you claim that birds migrate to the moon every winter."

Both men laughed, but the sheriff's voice grew serious. "But watch your ampersand. I'm only one man, and there's still plenty of hotheaded 'regulators' in Arkansas that just might try to jerk you to Jesus."

"I'll definitely keep that in mind, Sheriff. It does seem odd, though—it's clear you're suspicious of the Ravenels, but what about the Sloan brothers and their skinny cousin? That's a hard-looking outfit."

"Now, don't get fact mixed up with stupid. I've known them for years. Mostly they're just drunken bachelors who like to cut up rough when they're in town. Usually they just shoot at the moon."

"All due respect, Sheriff, but I don't get that impression. I've been sizing up frontier troublemakers for most of my life, and those three strike me as stone-cold killers, not just drunks who like to hurrah the town. And it appears to me that you coddle them."

"Don't let my manner fool you, Fargo. A sheriff is elected, not appointed, so I try not to have a dog in the fight. Some men come out west to escape injustice, others to escape justice. A town lawman has to be careful because it ain't always easy to tell them apart."

"I can't gainsay that," Fargo admitted.

"If it'll set your mind at ease," Jeffries added, "I don't consider the Sloan boys and Scout above suspicion. Hell, I once bent a gun barrel over Butch's head to stop him from shooting a teamster. And Scout Langley may be a lunger, but he's plenty dangersome. But I know for a fact that all three were right here in town during the latest heist, and the Ravenel boys were spotted on the stage road just before the holdup."

Sheriff Jeffries swung his solid bulk up into leather. "Ravenels *or* Sloans—I wouldn't take a cup of cold piss for the whole caboodle. Jessie excepted, of course. I meant the male side of the clan."

The sheriff pointed up toward the shattered window frame, a few jagged shards of glass reflecting in the moonlight. "Don't know's I blame you for having blood in your eye, Fargo. But this town is my jurisdiction. Let me handle it."

"I sure will," Fargo lied. He had never turned personal vendettas over to a star-packer in his life, and he saw no reason to start now. Especially with a man who made excuses for the Sloan outfit.

"Good. I can't arrest every man who falls foul of the law. I got a tiny jail and I don't worry overmuch about every stolen chicken or go-as-you-please fistfight—or stray Indian," he added, looking at Cranky Man. "But attempted murder I won't abide, Mr. Fargo. I'll do my level best to track the culprit down."

The sheriff reined his buckskin around and faded into the darkness.

"You believe him?" Cranky Man asked.

"Right now I don't know what to believe. He sounds sincere, but he didn't ask one question about what happened."

"Seems like a smart man, though."

"That he does," Fargo agreed. "That's what worries me."

Despite a severe lack of sleep, Fargo was awake at sunup. He washed, dressed, buckled on his gun belt, and sheathed his boot knife. He hurried over to the livery and climbed up into the loft, his nose wrinkling at the smell, and kicked Cranky Man's leg.

"Up and on the line, you worthless savage."

Cranky Man stirred slowly to life. "Rot in hell, Fargo."

"Christ Almighty, it smells like a mash vat in here."

Cranky Man groaned. "Not so loud, hair face."

Fargo spied an empty jug in the hay. "Whew! Homemade moonshine. How much of that did you drink?"

"Well, see, me and Dolomite split it half and half. But my half was on the bottom, and I had to help him with his half to reach mine."

Fargo said, "Right about now you must have a brick in your hat, old son."

Cranky Man struggled to sit up. "I feel like a sick oyster at low tide."

"Tough tit," Fargo snapped. "If horseshit was brains, you'd have a clean corral. I told you to be ready to saddle up at any time. Get your moccasins on and have a good puke because we're riding out."

Fargo climbed back down and found Dolomite sweeping out his small office with a sage broom. "Morning, Dolomite. How you feeling?"

"Awright, Mr. Fargo," he lied, forcing a weak smile.

"I see. Well, I got a bottle in my saddlebag—care for a morning bracer?"

Dolomite grimaced. "Nuh-un! Me 'n' that crazy Indian up in the hayloft done for a whole jug of moonshine. I feels like I done died and went to hell."

"Be careful of Cranky Man," Fargo warned. "He'd corrupt a priest."

"I know *that's* real. Mr. Fargo, your stallion's feet's all trim now, and that loose shoe on tight."

"Thanks, Dolomite. Say, have you heard of Butch and Romer Sloan and their cousin Scout?"

"Ax me has I heard o' cholera and the yellow vomit."

"I see you do know them. Know where they live?"

"Got 'em a shack few miles due south o' town, just off Turk Road. Ain't no road, really, just a growed-over wagon lane."

Fargo thanked him and lugged his tack out to the paddock, whistling in the Ovaro, who bumped his nose into Fargo's chest in greeting. After rigging his own horse, he tacked Cranky Man's skewbald.

"Put a wiggle on!" Fargo shouted up into the loft. "I don't mollycoddle drunks. You asked for this job—now drag your ass down here or I'll *kick* it down the ladder."

Cranky Man struggled down the wooden rungs, missing one of the lower ones and sprawling on his back in the dirt. Dolomite had strong black coffee brewed, and Fargo forced the Choctaw to drink two cups.

"Where we headed?" he asked when he saw his saddled horse.

"Wherever the trail leads us," Fargo replied. "We're gonna start with a boot print in front of the saloon. That's why I rousted you out so early—I don't want those prints covered over."

Both men forked leather and rode through the mostly empty street to the saloon. Fargo leaned out of the saddle and quickly located the boot print.

"The left heel leaves a ridge where a chunk of the boot is missing," Fargo told his friend. "C'mon, they lead into the alley beside the Razorback."

Fargo followed the track through the alley. About ten feet behind the saloon stood the rock dike holding back a talus slope. He found no sign that a horse had been hobbled, but the boot prints turned to the right.

"Just like I figured," he said. "During daylight it wouldn't be all that hard to climb the slope. It's only about thirty feet high, and a careful man could find solid footholds. But at night, especially if he wanted to skedaddle fast, he might start a slide."

"That rings right," Cranky Man agreed. "But why not leave his horse close by for a quick getaway?"

"Whoever tried to blow me to smithereens didn't want to leave an obvious trail. He doesn't know about his boot heel and figured the prints would just mingle with all the others. I'd wager we'll find signs where a horse waited as soon as the rock dike ends."

They followed the ridged boot prints—which were widely spaced as if by a running man—for another hundred yards or so. The dike ended, and sure enough, Fargo found still-flattened grass where a horse had been hobbled. Fargo poked a stick into droppings the horse had left.

"Still fresh inside," he said. "And the grass inside the prints hasn't sprung all the way back up yet. These were made maybe five or six hours ago at the most. This is our man."

The rider had cleared out fast, his mount's hooves tossing up divots of dirt and grass, and the trail was easy to follow. But Fargo was more worried about the terrain. Only a few days' ride west of there, the country was so wide open there was no way to distinguish near from far, and an ambush nearly impossible. But in this corner of Arkansas the infinite variety of the terrain was a dry-gulcher's paradise.

"Keep your eyes skinned," he warned Cranky Man. "They might be watching to see if we found the trail."

"Who's 'they'?"

"If I find a rattlesnake in my boot," Fargo replied, "I don't ask its name before I kill it. But right now this trail is headed toward the shack where the Sloan boys and their cousin live."

On their right, a slope covered with small jack pines made Fargo wary. But the lively bird chatter from that direction convinced him ambushers weren't lurking.

They covered another two miles or so, headed due south

through country dotted with pine trees and sliced by rocky gullies. Fargo suddenly raised his right hand.

"Small clearing ahead," he said. "Just hold tight while I take a look."

Fargo tossed the reins forward and dismounted, sliding his Henry from its boot. He leapfrogged from tree to tree until he reached the edge of the clearing.

A hastily knocked-together shack stood—or rather, leaned—at the far side of the clearing. There was only one window on the visible side, covered with oiled paper to keep out insects and let in light. Fargo spotted three sore-used horses in a makeshift corral behind the shack—none of which he recognized from the payroll heist three days ago. But a gang as well run as that one had been, Fargo figured, would be smart enough to use different horses for their crimes.

He whistled Cranky Man forward. The Choctaw brought his New Haven Arms rifle with him.

"This has got to be their diggin's," Fargo said. "It's right where Dolomite said it was. That narrow wagon lane on the right must be Turk Road."

Fargo picked a stiff weed and began picking his teeth with it, patiently watching the shack.

"So what now?" Cranky Man demanded.

"We could rush the shack," Fargo said from a deadpan face. "Kill them all."

Cranky Man's eyes bulged like wet, white marbles. "Has your brain come unhinged? I didn't mean anything like that."

"Don't be such a worrywart. You act like a Ponca, not a Choctaw."

Cranky Man saw Fargo's sly grin and realized he was being roweled. "Sure, crazy 'r' not, let's do it. Way my head feels, a bullet would be a curative."

Fargo shook his head. "We got a problem. The trail we followed proves that one man in that shack tried to kill me. But it doesn't prove this bunch are the holdup gang. After all, the way they see it, I turned some strutting roosters into capons yesterday at the saloon—in front of witnesses. That's reason enough to make scum buckets want to kill me."

"So what? From what I know of the Trailsman, *any* man who tries to murder him is marked for carrion bait."

"Not just any man, old son. It has to be the right man. I don't know which of those three wears that nicked boot."

"Christ, Fargo! You think all three didn't plan it out? Curs come in packs."

"Sure they did, but only one tried to do it. And you're forgetting something else—we saw five riders take that pay wagon, not just three. *If* this is part of the gang, which we haven't proved, there's at least two more we don't know about. My job is to find out all the names, and if we kill this bunch now we may never know who the other two are."

"That makes some sense," Cranky Man agreed. "Still, orders be damned. One of those chicken-plucking bastards tried to get your life over last night, Fargo. Don't seem right he just walks away like it's none of his picnic."

Fargo looked at his companion. "Once in a blue moon you get it right, you ugly red son. Before we go, I think I'll send in my card. Go back and wait with the horses—you're good at gentling them during gunfire, and we might need your rifle in reserve."

Since one of those mange pots had tossed black powder at Fargo, it seemed only fair to toss some lead back, and a 16-shot Henry was perfect for the job. He lowered the rifle's aperture a notch, sighting down to a hundred yards. As soon as Cranky Man had retreated, Fargo jacked a round into the chamber and sent a round through the oiled paper.

The sharp whip-crack of the rifle was amplified in the clear morning air. Levering and firing with methodical precision, Fargo emptied shot after shot into the flimsy shack. Each time he levered the breech, the ejector mechanism clicked flawlessly and a spent casing arced over his right shoulder.

A large water casket sat beside the plank door, its top dangling from a rope tether. Fargo sent his last two shots into the casket, leaks spouting just above the ground.

"Enjoy your morning coffee, boys," Fargo muttered.

Knowing retaliation would likely be swift, he dashed back toward the horses, expecting to find Cranky Man mounted and holding the Ovaro's reins for him. Instead, even as return fire opened up behind him and bullets chunked into the trees, he spotted Cranky Man's skewbald hopelessly tangled in its picket pin and fighting in a panic, eyes showing almost all whites.

"You damn knucklehead!" Fargo snapped. "Why didn't you use hobbles?"

"This bucket of glue won't tolerate hobbles. When you started firing, he got to crow-hopping and got twisted in the rope."

"Never mind kicking the damn pin out. Just cut the rope and untangle him."

The shots behind them got louder and more accurate as the occupants of the shack grew bolder, starting across the clearing. Fargo couldn't get to Cranky Man's saddle scabbard, so he drew his own sidearm and headed back to the tree line, bullets snapping past his ears. He spotted the Sloan brothers and Scout Langley, still in their long handles and all armed with repeating rifles. Sheltering as best he could, he sent them to the ground with three swift shots.

When Butch Sloan rose to his feet, Fargo snapped off the last three bullets in the wheel. But his enemies sensed their attackers were low on firepower and resumed the advance, dark blackpowder smoke hazing the air around them.

"Snap into it!" Fargo urged Cranky Man. Now the Trailsman resorted to his ace in the hole—the extra cylinder of ammo he carried in his possibles bag. He unscrewed the Colt's cylinder pin, the empty wheel falling into his hand, and quickly secured the new one. Fargo knew he had to rattle them to buy time, so he squeezed the trigger back and held it while he rapidly fanned the hammer, a flashy trick he used only in emergencies.

Fanning ruined accuracy, but the rapid explosions were unnerving and sounded like more than one shooter. All six of his bullets whipped through the tall weeds and forced the trio to eat dirt.

"Fargo!" Cranky Man called. "My line is free. Let's raise dust!"

"'Bout damn time," Fargo said, bolting into the trees.

He booted his Henry, vaulted into the saddle, and thumped the Ovaro with his heels. As they began their escape, a hammering racket of gunfire opened up behind them, slugs whiffing through the air all around them. Twice Fargo felt the wind-rip of lethally close bullets.

When they were well out of range, Fargo reined in and thumbed reloads into both the revolver cylinders.

"Think they'll follow us?" Cranky Man asked.

"Relax, old son. They likely don't even know about you yet. By the time they get dressed and tack their mounts, we'll be close to town. Besides, they know damn well it was me, anyhow, so they can make their play anytime."

"What's your next plan to get our lives over?" Cranky Man asked.

"I been studying on that," Fargo said, glancing at the sun. "It's still early in the forenoon. We've got plenty of time."

"For what?"

"It's like this: Colonel Mackenzie is a stuffed shirt, but he's no fool. He also strikes me as strict but fair. If he suspects the Ravenel clan of those payroll heists, he must have a reason for it. Jessie doesn't have to be at work for hours yet. Let's get her and take a ride out to the Ravenel farm."

"Why do we need the girl? You that horny?"

"Because this is Arkansas, you chowderhead, not Ohio. Around here, lead tends to fly when strangers ride up. Besides, what's my excuse for visiting if I don't have Jessie along?"

"Hell, the one brother knows you."

"Maybe he won't be the first one to spot me. And what if *you're* the first one they spot, red man?"

Cranky Man mulled that. "Yeah, I take your drift. They might think it's a bust out from the rez. For Christ sakes, let's get the girl."

7

As Fargo and Cranky Man trotted their mounts past the Razor-back Saloon, Fargo glanced up at his ruined window and saw that someone had covered it with thick boards, leaving a narrow slit for ventilation—and for Fargo to stick a gun barrel through.

"Seems like everybody always wants to kill you, Fargo," Cranky Man remarked. "You're one of those men who only has to show up to make enemies."

"Everybody? Women rarely try it," Fargo gainsaid. "They like me just fine."

"That gal Felicity, too, uh? She looked at you like you was dog shit on her new shoes."

"That one's a poser," Fargo admitted. "But that little filly can be broke to the saddle."

"Huh. Way she lords it around, you'd be lucky to sniff her dirty dainties."

Fargo grinned. "Maybe I'll get you something frilly."

They reached the hotel and tied off their mounts at the rail out front. Fargo had to be careful of Jessie's reputation, so he called over a young boy loafing on the boardwalk and paid him two bits to send up for her.

While he waited, Fargo moved behind the Ovaro's shoulder and took a good look around town. "If the Sloan boys and their skinny cousin are in town, they're not in the streets. But we'll be huggin' soon."

A Concord coach pulled by six horses pulled up to the hotel, so crowded that two dust-powdered men were sharing the rear dickey seat atop the coach. The messenger rider took one look at Cranky Man and swung the twin barrels of his sawed-off express gun at him.

"He's all right," Fargo called out. "We're U.S. Army scouts."

The man eyed Fargo and lowered the gun. "Well, *you* look like a scout, mister. That blanket ass looks like a sorry-ass reservation buck."

The sudden emergence of Felicity Meadows from the front door of the hotel broke the tension. She was dressed to the nines and smartly coiffed. Fargo took in her royal blue dress with velvet-trimmed cuffs and again wondered how a saloon singer afforded such luxury.

She headed straight for the boardwalk, shading herself with a silk parasol, and Fargo removed his hat. "Good morning, Miss Meadows."

When she cut him completely, pretending he wasn't even there, Fargo stepped boldly into her path. "Miss Meadows, I do wish you'd stop giving me the frosty mitt."

"Oh, you do? That just cuts me all to ribbons."

Her tone squashed any rejoinder, but Fargo pressed doggedly on. "I see you're not dressed for . . . riding. That's a fine chestnut you own."

Something in Fargo's tone, and vaguely implied meaning, seemed to sink through to her. Her nimbus-gray eyes deigned to meet his gaze, and this time when she spoke, her words were sweet in tone but brutally disparaging.

"I own many fine things, Mr. Fargo, unlike you who dress in crude animal skins and sport bullet holes in your dusty hat. I believe the quaint term 'trail bum' would apply."

At least she knew his name—Fargo found that interesting.

"It's what's under the clothes that matters," he said, his innuendo clear.

This was too much for Cranky Man, who burst out laughing, then assumed the face of a wooden Indian.

"No, Mr. Fargo, it's what's in a man's bank account that matters to me. And, therefore, you don't matter to me."

"Oh, I'd matter," he assured her, "once I plucked off those fine feathers of yours. I'd make it matter so much you couldn't stop thinking about it."

For the first time Fargo saw her nonplussed. "You certainly are brazen," she told him.

"No, I just know what I'm good at, and I see no reason to hide my lights under a bushel."

Some of the cold hostility in her face transformed itself into a budding curiosity. She placed her free hand lightly on her hip, seeming to really see him for the first time. "Well . . . I wonder."

Abruptly, she walked away.

"Fargo, you're a damned hound," Cranky Man said. "I'd a bought a ticket for *that* show."

"Don't be so sure it was just my good looks and charm," Fargo said.

"T'hell with that. It was your bawdy talk. She never hears such things, and it got her hot and bothered."

"It's possible," Fargo conceded. "No man alive can read sign on a woman's breast."

"Skye!"

"Speaking of a woman's breast," Cranky Man said, watching Jessie approach from the hotel, "here comes two more. Damn, those are sockdologers—I like a woman who jiggles when she walks. How does that little gal keep from falling on her face?"

"Stow it," Fargo snapped, aware that he now faced a dilemma. He had to give Jessie a convincing reason for wanting to visit her family, and he didn't have one.

"Howdy, handsome," she greeted him, slanting a curious glance at Cranky Man.

"Miss Jessie Ravenel, meet Cranky Man. He's ugly as a mud fence and has less get-up than a gourd vine. But he's been a strong right arm to me, when he's sober, and if there's trouble he's a good man to take along."

Jessie couldn't match the finery of Felicity's wardrobe, but she looked fetching in a sprigged-muslin dress with ribbon trims. She wore her chestnut hair in two thick plaits.

"Pleased to meetcha, Cranky Man," she said, flashing him a smile. "And Skye is full of it—you're *not* ugly. There's real character in your face."

"Thank you, ma'am. And may I say that you have a mighty fine pair of"—Fargo elbowed his ribs hard—"uh, eyes."

Jessie sent Fargo a puzzle-headed look. "I'm powerful glad to see you, Skye, but is something wrong?"

"Not at all, lady. Are you in the mood for a brief ride into the country?"

Her face brightened. "A picnic."

"Actually, I was hoping we could ride out to your farm."

"Whatever for? There ain't much to see but dry fields and sick livestock."

Fargo gave a long, fluming sigh. "I might's well just be honest since I can't think of a good lie. I'm s'posed to keep this dark, so I'll have to trust you not to say anything. You see—"

"You're working for the army, trying to get information on these holdups lately," she finished for him.

Fargo looked at Cranky Man. "You been shooting off your big mouth, Chief Soaring Eagle?"

"Go piss up a rope, Fargo. I ain't said a word—"

"Hesh down, both of you," Jessie cut in. "Skye, nobody had to tell me. Laws! Why else would the Trailsman, who works plenty for the army, ride into a jerkwater like Pine Hollow for a 'loafing spell'? And bein's there's a rumor my brothers is mixed up in it, naturally you need to poke into it."

"Right as rain," Fargo said. "But I have *not* come to any conclusions about your brothers. It's just, I'm under orders to take a closer look."

"A body don't need to worry about you being fair, Skye. And don't worry—I won't tell your secret to nobody. Well, I'm ready if you are."

Fargo turned the stirrup, swung up into leather, then slid forward against the horn and hoisted Jessie up behind him. "Hold on tight," he told her.

"Oh, I plan to, Mr. Fargo."

She was as good as her word, pressing her ample charms tight into Fargo's back. She giggled when he had to adjust himself in the saddle.

"Too bad we have to waste it," she whispered in his ear.

"Plenty more where that came from," he assured her.

As they left town, Cranky Man riding about twenty feet behind, Fargo searched the terrain all around them.

"Tell me something," he said to Jessie. "Would that gal Lynette take money to spy on me?"

"That strumpet would beat up a nun for a nickel. I spoze she's still offering her favors?"

Fargo nodded. "Seems to be a crusade with her."

"I don't wonder—nobody misses a slice off a cut loaf, and *that* loaf's been sliced plenty."

"Lynette, huh?" Cranky Man called up to them. "She do business with Indians?"

"Prob'ly," Jessie replied. "But you'd be shot for going into a white man's cathouse."

"If she is spying on me," Fargo pressed, "who would be paying her?"

"I don't rightly know, Skye. Us dance girls don't truck with the harlots. I'd have to study on it."

"Could Felicity have put her up to it?"

"Felicity? La! Whatever for? You may be the best-looking man in town, but she don't seem to cotton to you. She's mighty highfalutin, and you don't dress like one of the big bugs."

"All true," Fargo agreed, dropping the matter.

The day heated up rapidly, and deerflies pestered the Ovaro and Cranky Man's Indian scrub. Both men waved their hats now and then to scatter them.

"Almost there," Jessie said. "Next holler over."

Fargo had noticed a few dugouts and sheds, always in the distance, marking rustic dwellings. He heard a gulping sound behind him and looked back in time to see Cranky Man imbibing from his hip flask.

"This morning you were begging for a grave," Fargo reminded him.

"Hair off the dog, paleface, hair off the dog. Hangover's almost gone."

"My brothers are moonshiners," Jessie said, looking back at Cranky Man. "And they got no gripe agin Indians, so you'll have plenty to drink."

"Don't encourage him," Fargo pleaded.

"I ought better warn you, though," she added. "My pa fought Choctaws starting back in Mississippi, and I ain't rightly sure how he'll take to having one in the house."

"Any chance he'll shoot him?" Fargo asked.

"Not hardly."

"Damn the luck," Fargo said.

"Fargo," Cranky Man groused, "I love you, too, you son of a bitch. Sorry, Miss Ravenel—I meant son of a buck."

"There's home," Jessie announced as they topped a dusty hill. "Ain't much to brag on, is it?"

The farm was nestled in a wide, slightly hilly valley, the dry fields forming a circle around a low, pine-log house and a scattering of outbuildings. Fargo took in a scratch-penny herd of a half-dozen cows, ribs showing like barrel staves. As they rode nearer he saw a plow with rusty shares lying in the front yard, and a little shirttail patch of kitchen vegetables grew along one side of the house.

Jessie, Fargo reflected, had already admitted her brothers were moonshiners. But the senior Ravenel owned title to six hundred acres, and land taxes were high in Arkansas. Would moonshine profits even cover the tax, or would more drastic crimes be necessary?

As they neared the house, four men stepped out into the yard, armed to the teeth. The obvious patriarch looked to be straight out of Genesis. He was long-jawed, had an old hickory-nut face, eyes like a pair of open wounds, and held a Hunt repeating rifle aimed at Cranky Man.

"I brung company, Pa!" Jessie sang out.

"Boys," the old man said, "don't shoot the redskin until we know where his squaw lives."

Cranky Man's jaw dropped open, and all four men burst into raucous laughter.

"Don't fret, John," Pa Ravenel said. "We're just joshing you. Injun or white, iffen you're a friend of one of ourn, then you're a friend of the clan."

"If there's a virgin in this bunch," Cranky Man muttered to Fargo, "it's only because she runs faster than her brothers."

"Pipe down, you fool," Fargo warned. "Talk like that will get both of us an ass full of Blue Whistlers."

Fargo dismounted and helped Jessie down.

"Skye Fargo and Cranky Man," she said, "this here's my pa, Elijah, and my brothers Lindsay, Taylor, and Jake. That's Esther, my ma, poking her head out the kitchen door. She's a mite bashful."

Elijah said, "Mr. Fargo, Jake told us what you done at the saloon, and we're beholden."

He looked at his wife. "Ma, scare up some grub. Jake, tend to the horses."

Jake led both men to an open-face shed and forked hay into a canvas net while they loosened the girths and threw the bridles.

All three new arrivals washed up in soft cistern water and headed toward the kitchen door. Near the house a rotting plank served as a bridge across a ditch filled with muddy water.

Everyone else made it across effortlessly, but Cranky Man had drained his flask in the saddle and made a misstep. He belly flopped into the mud soup and came up cussing like a stable sergeant.

The Ravenel males again howled with mirth. "Look, Pa!" shouted Lindsay. "I thought he was a Choctaw, but he must be Apache—a Messy Apache!"

"Mescalero," Fargo clarified when Jessie gave him a puzzled look.

"I seen clay-colored Injins," Taylor added, "but nary mud!"

Ma Ravenel came scolding out the kitchen door. "You rapscallions hesh up! He's Jessie's friend and a guest in our house. I'll not see you mockin' him."

"Ma's ezactly right, boys," Elijah said. "Just hold your taters. Crotchety Man ain't Christian, but we are so whack the cork."

"It's *Cranky* Man," the Choctaw protested, muddy water pouring off him in rivulets.

Fargo, still laughing, pulled his sullen-faced friend out, and Ma Ravenel led him to a hand pump near the house. The rest trooped into the house through a large kitchen with cross-stitch samplers on every wall and a rusty cookstove sitting on brick legs.

"This here's Cindy, the youngest," Jessie said, indicating a girl of eleven or twelve. She sat on a stool in one corner, moving the dasher of a churn up and down to bring butter.

Elijah led the way into a messy room too squalid to call a parlor. He pointed to a rawhide-patched chair and Fargo sat down, aware the Ravenel men were watching him as they might a circus curiosity. Jessie sat down in a nearby rocking chair, the rest on three-legged stools or old powder kegs—quite a few powder kegs, Fargo noted.

"Jessie tells me the drought has hit you folks hard," he told Elijah.

"Hard? Mr. Fargo, we're runnin' hard just to stand still. I got half a mind to tie a cow to the end gate and move on. Leave the hull damn shootin' match for squatters."

"Rain could be better this summer," Fargo said. "It's early

yet. I took a look at some spiderwebs a few days back. They're spinning their strands thick—that usually means plenty of rain coming."

Pa Ravenel's face came alive with interest. "Why, that's so, ain't it? I plumb forgot. Anyhow, right now it's Jessie's wages keepin' us alive—that, and some exter the boys pick up brewin' mash."

While this conversation went forward, Fargo watched Taylor Ravenel return to the kitchen and come back with a lead ladle, pouring its hot contents into a bullet mold sitting on a stool. With the exception of the old man's rifle, all the weapons Fargo could see were single-shot long guns and cap-and-ball pistols—nothing matching the repeating weapons used in the heist three days ago. And the only horses he'd spotted outside were big dobbins, gentle workhorses.

Assuming, Fargo reminded himself, that better weapons and horses weren't stashed somewhere else.

"Here's the noble red man," Taylor quipped as Ma Ravenel led a sheepish-looking Cranky Man into the room. He wore one of the boy's old shirts and trousers, so big they made him look like a scarecrow, and his wet hair was plastered back.

Fargo looked a warning at the Choctaw, who somehow bit his tongue. Esther returned to the kitchen. Elijah passed Cranky Man a jug of home brew, and he brightened considerably. The rest stared in astonishment as he took it down like sugar water and smacked his lips.

"Now *that's* medicine," he proclaimed.

"Goldang," Jessie remarked. "That feller has a cast-iron stomach. That whiskey could raise blood blisters on a saddle."

"Mr. Fargo," Jake said, "I would like to seen Butch Sloan's ugly face when you put him under the gun."

"Why di'n't you plug the son of a bitch?" Lindsay added.

"Launder your talk, boy," Elijah said mildly. "They's a woman present."

"Beg pardon, sis."

Elijah pulled a plug from his coveralls, sliced off a chew, and soon had it juicing proper. "Mr. Fargo, I keep tellin' these knot-headed boys of mine—a man can't always stand up for his honor or he'd never stop fighting. They're all hell-bent on a showdown with the Sloan boys and their cousin."

Fargo saw an opening here. "I talked to Sheriff Jeffries about that bunch. It's hard to draw a bead on him. The man's friendly, and I'd say he has a good think-piece. But he seems to think those three are all gurgle and no guts."

Elijah mulled that, then cheeked his wad. "I got no use for any lawman, nor any guv'ment, neither. But I'll allow as how Cody Jeffries ain't the worst badge-toter I've knowed. He knows we sell moonshine but pretends he *don't* know. That's mighty white of him."

"*Mighty* white," Cranky Man chimed in, imitating Elijah's drawl.

Pa Ravenel watched Cranky Man in silence, then looked at Fargo. "Mite tetched, is he?"

"Crazy as a pet coon."

"Anyhow, it's kinder funny about Cody," Lindsay said. "A sheriff's paid thirty dollars a month, yet Cody's got money to toss at the birds."

"His people's rich," Jessie pointed out.

"Could be," Elijah said. "Or might be just him what's rich. I ain't never seen these rich kin."

"Well, he's flat-out wrong about the Sloan boys and their lunger cousin," Jake said. "He *knows* them three is sons of trouble, but he just gives them free rein. He didn't use to be like that."

"You folks think that bunch are involved in these holdups lately?" Fargo asked.

"I'd bet my horse it's them," Jake attested. "But there's them hereabouts as hopes to see us Ravenel boys swing for it."

"The boy's speaking God's truth, Mr. Fargo," Elijah said, passing the jug to Fargo. "Our clover is thinning out. This country still had the Lord's thumbprint fresh on it when we first settled here. Why, you could leave your hoe in the dirt overnight, and next morning you'd find grapes growing out the handle."

Cranky Man, who had never tilled soil, suddenly lost his bored look and leaned forward. "Purple grapes?"

"Pink," Elijah said from a deadpan face. "With silver polka dots."

The entire room exploded in laughter and Cranky Man scowled.

"You gullible simp," Fargo chided him.

"Hell, it ain't even funny," Cranky Man said. "I didn't believe that overnight grapes stuff."

"My red friend," Elijah said, "little is left the poor man except humor. You need to belly laugh more."

Fargo feared Cranky Man's retort, but Ma Ravenel saved the day by calling from the kitchen, "Vittles is ready."

Fargo squeezed in between Jake and Jessie at a rough puncheon table with no cloth and two long benches for seats. Ma had set out fried grits, bacon, pan bread and a dewberry cobbler for dessert.

"Ma puts out good grub when she can," Elijah bragged as he heaped his plate. "Mr. Fargo, you ain't no apron-tied man, I'd wager."

"Bet he's *un*-tied a few," Lindsay cracked, and the boys sniggered while Jessie blushed crimson.

"Lindsay!" Ma Ravenel snapped.

Fargo noticed her face had been enfolded in worry since he'd arrived, and he suspected he knew why. Her next remark proved him right.

"'Tain't funny," she huffed. "It's *sin* you're laughing at. Your sweet sister, dancin' in a saloon!"

"You and your dang starched corset," Elijah said around a mouthful of food. "Jessie's wages are keepin' this family alive. So what iffen she dances with men? She could be doin' things a powerful lot worse with 'em."

"How do we know she ain't? Temptation can ruin even a good girl like her. She's got a room in town."

"I live with another girl, Ma. Pattie. She's a good girl."

"I reckon Mr. Fargo has his own room. He seems like a gentleman, but he's powerful handsome and ... anyhow, next it will be the boys, besotted with Jezebels and Demon Rum."

"Crying out loud, Ma," Jake put in, "we make moonshine."

"That's for medicine purposes."

"Powerful medicine," Cranky Man agreed. "I'm hoping for another dose."

Fargo had paid close attention to this little family drama, and it had answered an important question for him: was Jessie's job, and the family's poverty, all an act to cover for the holdups? The comments by Ma Ravenel, however, and her tortured face, were not an act. This family was hurting, and Jessie's job was no diversion. For Fargo, his hunch had become a fact—the Ravenel boys were not likely part of the holdup gang.

Fargo looked at Esther Ravenel, read the pain in her eyes, and decided to lie his ass off. "Mrs. Ravenel, perhaps you should know that I'm a Mormon. As an unmarried man, I'm forbidden to . . . know any woman before marriage. Strictly forbidden. Jessie and I are good friends, but nothing more."

Cranky Man choked on a swallow of food.

"By the horn spoons!" Elijah exclaimed. "Straight arrow?"

"Straight arrow, old roadster," Fargo assured him. He had chosen the lie, now he must give it his all.

Ten years seemed to melt away from Ma Ravenel's face, while Jessie struggled to hold back laughter. The boys—especially Jake—looked dubious, but discreetly stayed quiet. They knew the lie was for their mother's sake.

"As a religious man," Ma said, "this will amaze you. Little Cindy here knows the Lord's Prayer so good she can recite it backwards. Show him, sugar babe."

Fargo was indeed amazed as the little girl rapidly rattled off the prayer in reverse. Everyone applauded.

"Now, just a minute," Cranky Man said. "If saying it frontwards can get white folks into heaven, won't saying it backward send that little girl straight to hell?"

At this blasphemy a shocked silence filled the kitchen. The brothers all laid down their forks, staring granite-faced at Cranky Man.

"Humor is all we have," he reminded them. "Have a good belly laugh."

Little Cindy's face looked like it had been drained by leeches. "Ma, am I going to hell?" she blubbered.

"Cranky Man," Fargo said lightly, "that acid tongue of yours don't help your disposition none."

"I got no interest in helping it."

"Yeah, I've noticed. Apologize to that little girl, you numbskull, or I'll whip you until your hair falls out."

But Pa Ravenel's sense of humor solved the crisis. He suddenly shook with laughter, slapping his thigh. "Ah, that redskin's off his head, boys, take no offense. He don't understand what he's sayin'. Injins're likable enough cusses, but they got no more sense than a turnip."

"That's for sure," Fargo said, sending Cranky Man a quelling stare. "But this one's going to wise up mighty quick."

8

Eyes slitted against the westering sun, holding the Ovaro to an easy trot, Fargo watched the scant-grown hills surrounding them. It was hard to remain vigilant with Jessie pressing herself against him and nibbling on his ear.

"Can I come see you again tonight?" she whispered.

"Lady, if I was ever tempted. But it's not safe in my room. You heard that explosion last night."

"Where, then?"

"Believe me, I'll be working on that plan."

She sighed. "I'll be thinking about it all night at work. Skye?"

"Hmm?"

"This visit to my place today—didja find out what you needed to know?"

Fargo nodded. "That I did. Your brothers are off my list, Jessie. Not that they were ever really on it."

"Told you so. They're a mite wild—'specially Jake—and they got no use for tin stars. But holdups is outta their line."

They rode through a streambed littered with boulders, and abruptly Fargo felt the back of his neck tingle. But the Ovaro showed none of his usual danger signals. Fargo carefully studied their surroundings, seeing nothing more dangerous than a badger digging a burrow.

Cranky Man rode up beside them. Ma Ravenel had wrapped his wet and muddy clothing into a bundle tied with twine, and it was lashed behind his saddle. Fargo hadn't said a word to him since they'd left the farm.

"Jesus, you're a holy show," he said now. "You just always have to upset the cart, don't you?"

"The hell you bellyachin' about?" Cranky Man demanded.

"I just hope you're proud. Making a sweet little girl think

she's going to hell. I don't mind your lip, but Jessie's folks fed you, gave you liquor, and then you pissed on their boots."

"Ahh, maybe it's not the brightest thing I've done all year," Cranky Man admitted. "I wasn't trying to make your sister feel bad, Jessie. It's just my contrary nature."

"Well, Skye ought to talk," Jessie said. "Making hisself out to be a Mormon. Least Cranky Man didn't tell no lies."

"No," Fargo said, "but I saw the sneaky pup steal an envelope."

"An envelope? What—?"

"Shush it," Fargo ordered, for the Ovaro's ears had just pricked forward. Realizing they were all only moments away from death, he swept Jessie unceremoniously out of the saddle and into a sandy gully.

"Christopher Columbus!" she cried in shock.

"Lie down flat," Fargo ordered. "Don't move until I tell you to."

Fargo loosened the Henry in its saddle scabbard. "We got a fox play coming," he warned Cranky Man. "Get a wiggle on or we're all going to glory!"

Both men gigged their horses forward just as rapid gunfire erupted from a brushy ridge on their left flank. Fargo led his friend into the nearest cover, a stand of mulberry trees.

"Fargo, these damn trees are skinny," Cranky Man complained as bullets rained in nineteen to the dozen.

"All we got until I grow some more, old son," Fargo replied while he swung down and jerked his Henry out. "Tie your horse short or he'll bust loose."

Fargo dropped into a kneeling offhand position and levered his rifle. "Don't waste ammo," he said. "Only shoot if you can spot powder smoke."

The two men were only partially protected by trees, and their position was precarious. Adding to their troubles, a stiff wind was dispersing their attackers' smoke.

"It's no good," Fargo said. "From the sound, I estimate four, prob'ly five shooters. See that line of wild plum and choke-cherry bushes about a hundred feet ahead of us. It'll be better than this spot. I'll throw down cover fire while you go first."

"Christ, it's open ground between here and there. Our hash is cooked!"

"Nerve up. This is pee doodles beside other scrapes we've been in. *Go!*"

Fargo began peppering the ridge, hot brass shell casings clattering into the tree. Despite Cranky Man's Doomsday pronouncements, Fargo knew he was a stalwart fighter, and he made a mad, zigzagging run for the cover ahead, his rifle at a high port.

The moment he dove to safety, Cranky Man's New Haven Arms repeater started cracking as he covered Fargo. The Trailsman sprinted out from cover. He felt the wind-rip of several bullets, one tugging at a pants leg, but dove to Cranky Man's side unscathed.

This position was better, but still provided poor cover from the volume of lead tearing into them.

"The hell we doing?" Cranky Man demanded. "They got the high ground, and you said there's four or five of them. We shoulda just hightailed it when they opened fire."

"I don't expect a red son to care about the code out here," Fargo replied, shooting when he spied muzzle flash. "But it's Jessie who guides our actions now. They'd likely have shot her off my horse before we got clear, so I put her in good cover. Now we have to run these sage rats off to keep her safe."

A bullet ricocheted off the Henry's brass frame, dinging it.

"Yeah, that shines," Cranky Man said. "Same with the red man's code: women and children first. I'm too nerve-frazzled to think straight."

"You're doing fine," Fargo assured him. "Never panic—that's the main mile. This is a tight scrape, but if we stay frosty and shoot plumb we'll rout 'em. These are back-shooting cowards, not Choctaw warriors."

Cranky Man was out of loads for his rifle, and pulled the Dragoon from his belt. Fargo heard the Henry's hammer click on an empty chamber.

"Give me that," he said, taking the Dragoon. He pulled his belt gun, giving it and the spare cylinder to Cranky Man. "Take the shell belt, too. You've got twelve shots before you need to reload. When you fire all twelve, just open this loading gate and thumb the reloads in."

Fargo removed his hat and shirt, rigging them up in the bushes.

"The hell you up to?" Cranky Man demanded.

"This is my buckskin-man trick. I want them thinking we're both still down here."

"You mean we're pulling foot?"

"No, you damn fool. You stay here and keep up as much fire as you can. I'm taking this hand cannon and hooking around their left flank. With luck, hearing a Dragoon open up at short range will rout these milk-livers."

Fargo started to leave, but Cranky Man caught his arm. "If I get killed, Fargo, and you make it, will you make sure I'm buried faceup?"

Fargo nodded. Although Cranky Man had abandoned his tribe and most of the tribal ways he still believed that an Indian buried facedown could never see the Place Beyond the Sun.

"You won't get killed," Fargo assured him. "Only the good die young."

Bent low, using the bushes as cover, Fargo first ran to his right. No bullets chased him, so his buckskin decoy must have worked. When the bushes thinned out, he began leapfrogging up the face of the ridge, using boulders, runoff seams, any cover he could find. Unrelenting fire continued from the attackers, but Cranky Man did a fair job of sounding like two men firing back.

Moving in, gnats swarmed his sweaty face. Despite his brave talk to rally Cranky Man, Fargo knew they were both up against it. If he was wrong, and this surprise probe failed to rout the enemy, only five bullets stood between him and death.

But Fargo had perfectly calculated his enemy. When no more cover was available to him, he opened up with a thunderous boom of the Dragoon, three close-spaced shots. He still could not see his well-hidden foes, but once they realized their flank was compromised, they beat a hasty retreat. Fargo could hear the brush rattling as they escaped. Taking a gamble, he ran forward and fired two more shots. Moments later, he heard the rataplan of escaping hooves.

Fargo, out of ammo, had to lie low in case a rear guard had been left behind to cover the escape. By the time he crested the ridge, he saw only an empty, rocky plateau sloping away from the ridge and merging with a pine forest below.

"Fargo! You still sassy?"

"Still in one piece," he called to Cranky Man. "But I didn't catch one glimpse of our friends. It was a perfect ambush position."

He joined his friend. Their faces were powder-blackened and showed the strain of battle.

"You plan to cut sign on them?" Cranky Man asked.

Fargo shook his head. "We'll have to let them take this trick. We need to get Jessie back to town in case they decide to counterattack."

"I wonder if it was that bunch we traded lead with this morning," Cranky Man said as they returned to their horses and mounted.

"Happens it was," Fargo pointed out. "They picked up a couple extra yellow curs."

"And there you got the five we saw a few days ago."

Fargo nodded. "I'd wager. But we didn't actually see them, so it could be the local vigilantes the sheriff warned us about."

"You believe that?"

"Nah. I don't think vigilantes would operate this smooth, and there'd likely be more of them—what they lack in guts they make up in numbers. This bunch that jumped us are some hard twists, all right, and they know how to set up an ambush. The kind of skill Scout Langley might have."

Jessie, still covered down in the gully, rose to her feet as they approached. "La! It did give my heart a jupe when all them guns started to bark. I never heard so much shootin' at once. Are you two all right?"

Cranky Man thumped his chest. "Me heap big Chief Soaring Eagle."

Jessie bit her knuckles, still clearly agitated. Fargo felt a stab of guilt as he pulled her up behind him. "It's over," he assured her. "I was stupid to take you with us. It won't happen again."

"Now I see what your life is like," she said. "How can you stand it?"

Fargo gave her an over-the-shoulder look, mustering a grin. "Actually, lady, I enjoy a good set-to. But not when I drag a woman into it."

"But he doesn't care how many Choctaws he gets killed," Cranky Man chimed in. "Maybe if I gussied up and wore a dress . . ."

"The hell you squawking about, heap big chief? You're still alive, damn the luck."

Cranky Man looked all around as they gigged their horses toward town. "Yeah, but this is Arkansas. That could change real quick."

Fargo left Jessie in front of the hotel, the afternoon sun lengthening his shadow in the street, and rode with Cranky Man to the livery at the opposite end of town. As they turned in at the yard, Fargo spotted Dolomite cleaning fish on a stump.

"*Lord* have mercy!" the liveryman said, glancing up at the two men's powder-smudged faces. "Either you gen'muns stuck your faces in a steam stack, or you bin in one catarumpus of a gun battle."

"Never mind us," Fargo said, lighting down and staring at Dolomite's bloody lips and swollen-shut left eye. "The hell happened to you?"

"Dickens take it all, Mr. Fargo. They was a couple mean-lookin' snakes here earlier wantin' to know when you rode out and which way."

"And I take it you didn't cooperate?"

"Nuh-un. I told them I ain't seed scratch nor hair of Fargo all day. I be damn I help them curly wolves."

"You know 'em?"

"Seen 'em around couple times, is all. Look like outlaw trash to me."

Fargo pulled his tack. "Well, you're a brave man, but from now on just talk out if you get threatened on my account. You know nothing that can hurt me, so just cooperate, all right?"

"Nuh-un. I won't, all due respeck. That riffraff can kill me on account the law say a black man cain't own a gun nor a horse— not even a dog. But I ain't a slave no more, and how I can look myself in the eye if I don't stand up like a man?"

Fargo and Cranky Man exchanged a glance while Dolomite began rubbing down the Ovaro with a handful of hay.

"Dolomite," Fargo said, placing a hand on his shoulder, "I'm proud to know you."

"Goes double for me," Cranky Man said gruffly, unused to kind words.

Fargo washed up at the water trough and grabbed a quick

meal at the Half Moon. He brought back a small pail of white beans and ham hocks for Dolomite and Cranky Man. Then he headed toward the Razorback, staying on the shady side of the street and keeping his eyes in motion. He pushed open the batwings. Business was still slow, but he knew the place would soon be packed.

"Dave," he said to the barkeep, "it's my fault Jessie's a little late. She'll be along shortly."

"Ain't much business right now, anyhow. You lucky stiff. Ain't she a little honey? So somebody tried to snuff your wick last night? The window's boarded up tight now. Listen . . ."

Dave leaned closer across the bar and lowered his voice. "Fargo, I don't go in for these horseshit rumors. But a new man in town is always the first to be blamed for everything from a swole-bellied woman to crop failures. There's a new rumor spreading about a vigilantes' reward for whoever kills you. Keep your eyes to all sides."

A vigilantes' reward . . . maybe, Fargo thought, the attackers earlier had also heard that rumor. More likely, they started it.

"Thanks, Dave. If the locals start to put the cootie on you for boarding me, just let me know and I'll pull up stakes."

"Ahh, nothing hurts my business. Say, I damn near forgot. See that soldier drinking by himself at the last table? He asked to see you. He's been here about an hour."

Fargo spotted a tall, lean, mustachioed cavalry trooper nursing a beer. As Fargo started back, the card sharper riffled a deck and called out, "Say, sport—how 'bout a friendly game of chance?"

The three men playing poker with him refused to look up at Fargo.

"Maybe some other time," Fargo dismissed him.

"Don't tarry too long. A man with a reward on his head has to live fast."

Fargo paused. "You're the big gambler. Slide that ladies' muff gun out of your sleeve and collect that reward now."

"Maybe some other time," the sharper mimicked Fargo.

"Don't tarry too long," Fargo mimicked him right back.

"Don't it beat the Dutch, gents?" the sharper called out in a taunting voice. "My daddy told me no man need bother coming west if he don't care for poker. I guess this gent prefers to stick with checkers."

No one laughed. Fargo's hard blue eyes bored into the loud mouth. "It's too bad your daddy didn't also teach you the difference between skill and cheating. Or between a man and a greasy, spineless weasel."

The pasteboard artist remained unperturbed. "You're implying a serious charge, chappie. I say it's because you're scared to stack chips against me."

"I'll stack 'em," Fargo promised. "And I'll beat you on your own terms, limit game or table stakes."

The gambler flashed a tight-lipped smile. "You know where to find me."

Fargo crossed to the soldier's table. "Name's Fargo. Mind if I join you?"

"Sure, have a seat. I guessed you must be Fargo," the soldier said, "when I heard you and that white-livered gambler lock horns. I'm Private James Hargrove, sir, dispatch rider from Fort Bowman. Colonel Mackenzie sends his compliments."

Fargo spun a chair around backward and dropped onto it, resting his muscular forearms on the back. "You can bottle this 'sir' shit, Jim. I'm just a civilian. What's the word from Mackenzie?"

"He wants a report—anything you have for him so far. I'm to wait while you write it. Not to rush you, sir—I mean, Mr. Fargo—but the old man will have an ace-high shit fit if I don't deliver your report sometime tonight. And he's a grizz if I roust him out of bed too late."

Fargo snorted. "Old Fuss and Feathers . . . yeah, I've seen him when he's in a pucker, and it ain't pretty. Sure, trooper, I'll go upstairs right now and write it. While you wait for me, you in the mood for some slap and tickle?"

The dispatch rider's face brightened. "Oh, *hell* yes. I'm sick of those old squaws in Hog Town. It costs more here, though."

Fargo laid a gold dollar on the table. "Uncle Whiskers is paying for this one. Go upstairs and ask for Lynette. Tell her Fargo sent you to see how good she is. Be careful, though—that little firecracker might set your tallywhacker ablaze."

Trooper Hargrove hurried upstairs while Fargo borrowed

writing supplies from Dave. Upstairs in his room, he secured the door and dropped the writing supplies onto the bed. He slacked into the chair for a few minutes, scrubbing his face with his hands. The gun battle earlier, and a lack of sleep, left his muscles heavy and exhausted.

He switched to the bed and used the wooden chair for a writing surface:

Colonel Mackenzie—
Events are coming to a boil here. I've carried out your orders to look and listen, but my presence in town has Dame Rumor working night and day against me. I've had two shooting scrapes and two ambush attempts on my life.
It's my judgment you've been bamboozled about the Ravenel boys. These lads are what you call harum-scarum— wild and reckless, but not hidebound criminals. My best hunch right now is that two brothers named Butch and Romer Sloan, and their cousin Scout Langley, are part of the holdup gang.
But somebody else is the brains behind this bunch, and I'm still untying that knot. One poser is Sheriff Jeffries. He's tried to steer me toward the Ravenels and away from the other three. I plan to look into that a little closer.

Fargo

Fargo stuck the steel pen back in the ink pot and shook some sand off his hat to blot the page. He folded it, stuck it in an envelope, and melted some sealing wax to secure the fold. His lips eased back off his teeth in a grin as he listened to Lynette work the cavalryman into a whirling dervish of frenzied pleasure. Evidently her erotic expertise matched her brags. But, again, Fargo wondered who was paying her to seduce and watch him.

Fargo waited outside in the empty hallway. Hargrove practically staggered out of Lynette's room, still buckling his belt.

"Holy Christ, Mr. Fargo," he said in a stunned voice. "I'm gonna limp for life. I asked her to marry me, but she said there's no profit in it."

Fargo laughed. "She could buy and sell both of us—she's the top hand at this hog ranch. On a good night she clears twenty dollars for herself. Here, tuck this in your tunic," he added, hand-ing Hargrove the envelope. "I thought there was a telegraph in this burg?"

"There is, but the colonel doesn't trust it. See you next trip, Mr. Fargo, and thanks for the introduction to Lynette."

The Colonel doesn't trust it. Hargrove headed for the stairs while those words set Fargo to wondering.

"Right after you left, I saw the sheriff buffalo a drunk teamster and haul him to the calaboose," Cranky Man told Fargo. "He tried the peaceful way first, but the teamster threw a punch at him."

"Take more than a punch to drop Cody Jeffries," Fargo re-plied.

"You could lick him."

"Maybe, but I've lost my share of dustups."

The two men sat atop the top rail of the livery corral as day dozed into night. The steady breeze felt good after the stagnant heat of the day.

Two riders, shadowy outlines in the twilight, appeared from the outskirts of town. They reined in at the livery yard, and the oily yellow lamplight from the barn etched their faces—hard, cunning faces with violent purpose written all over them.

"Jump down and set your heels," Fargo warned. "I'd wager these are the two jackals who roughed up Dolomite today. And maybe the two who make five, if you take my drift."

"You Fargo?" demanded a rider wearing a low-crowned shako hat.

"Depends who's asking."

"I'm Baxter Sanford and this here is Jonas Wheeling, case it's any of your damn beeswax. We been appointed by some other concerned citizens to find out why that redskin is off the reser-vation. Arkansas law allows for no free-ranging Injins."

"Take it up with the sheriff," Fargo suggested. "I'm just a peace-loving citizen."

"We done that, weak sister. He said take it up with you."

"Well, take this up first. What authority do you have to whip on Dolomite Jones? He's a legally freed man."

"So you're a coon lover, too, hanh?" Jonas Wheeling said. He hawked up a wad of spit and tobacco and aimed it expertly at

Cranky Man's foot. "Ain't got no suption left. 'Baccy ain't worth shit when it's got no suption left."

"You cracker bastard." Cranky Man's hand started for the sheath behind his neck, but Fargo stopped him.

"Stay frosty, old son," Fargo muttered.

"I double hot-tie *dare* you to pull that blade, red ape. You'll be the sorriest son of a bitch in seventeen states."

"Well, shit-oh-dear, these hog-humpers are feeling frisky," Fargo told his friend. "Must be sorta frustrated after tossing all that lead at us today and scoring no kills. Buncha schoolgirls with squirrel guns coulda done a better job."

Fargo knew where this was headed. These men had come here to kill, and because of Fargo's reputation they were easing up to it slow, trying to nerve themselves up. He was goading them in his cool, amiable manner, riling them to a boil—enraged men made bad mistakes.

"Mister, you're plumb loco," Sanford said. "Iffen *we* tossed lead at you, you'd be feeding worms."

"Baxter, I'll bet you a dollar to a doughnut," Wheeling badgered, "that buckskin boy here thinks he's got a set of stones on him."

"Likely, Jonas. But I say he's a goddamn, shit-eating Indian lover. How do you like *them* apples, Fargo?"

Fargo laughed. "You're a *quaint* cockchafer, Baxter. I'll give you that. But I say I'd rather love an Indian than hump a sheep—but I'm sure you two boys disagree. I can smell the mutton from here."

There was enough light limning Baxter Sanford for Fargo to see his face purple and his jaw muscles bunch. "You best swallow back them words, mister. Elsewise, I'm gonna knock out your teeth and then kick you in the stomach for mumbling."

"Oww, that scorched," Fargo told Cranky Man. "These two are *some*."

He looked up at the two hard cases. Fargo's face was a mask of serenity—eerily out of place with his next remark. "I think you two goober peas best get square with your maker—the death hug's a-comin'."

The unexpected word "death," and Fargo's unnerving, indecipherable smile, made both men nervous. They switched their attention back to Cranky Man.

"*Look* at this sad sack of shit, Jonas," Baxter said. "Good for nothing but squaw work. Let's call him White Man Runs Him."

It was like a red rag to a bull. "Sorry, Fargo—it's past peace-piping now," Cranky Man muttered.

"Agreed, but don't kill him, hoss," Fargo whispered. "Just hurt him good. Sheriff's watching."

In a blur of speed, as Baxter slapped at his gun, Cranky Man unsheathed, tossed, and buried his six-inch obsidian blade deep in Baxter's thigh, making him yowl like a cat with a torn dew-claw. Jonas Wheeling, too, tried to jerk his belt gun, but Fargo grabbed him by the shirt and dragged him from the saddle. He landed in a crooked crouch, and the toe of Fargo's boot smashed hard into his groin. When he knelt in excruciating pain, cupping himself, Fargo's knee destroyed several of his front teeth and knocked him senseless.

By now the sheriff was hustling across the wide street.

"To hell with that law dog," Cranky Man said. "These ain't just bullyboys, they're kill crazy. Let's put 'em under."

Before Baxter could rally from his knife wound, Fargo pulled Baxter's six-gun and tossed it. He remembered Colonel Macken-zie's stern admonition not to play judge and executioner.

"'Fraid we can't," he told Cranky Man, watching the sheriff break into a run as he drew nearer. "But never you mind—we *will* be settling some accounts."

9

Sheriff Cody Jeffries surveyed the scene in the livery yard. Jonas Wheeling, still out cold, lay sprawled on his face. Baxter Sanford now sat on the ground, hissing from pain and trying, with trembling hands, to remove the deeply embedded knife in his thigh.

"All right, Fargo," Jeffries said in a weary tone, "self-defense, right?"

Fargo nodded. "Baxter there tried to clear leather, and Cranky Man beat him to the punch. When Jonas went for his shooter, I changed his mind for him."

Jeffries slanted an indifferent glance toward Jonas. "Is he dead?"

"Nah, I just cracked his nuts and extracted a few of his teeth. By rights, we *could* have killed both of them, Sheriff."

"He's a goddamn liar, Cody," Baxter managed, rocking back and forth in pain. "Me and Jonas just rode in to water our mounts, and these crazy sons of bitches jumped us for no reason."

"That's a bald-faced lie," Jeffries said. "The two of you weren't nowhere near the water trough—you rode right up to Fargo and the buck and started running your mouths."

Baxter started to respond, but just then Cranky Man bent down and jerked his knife loose. Baxter gave out a shrill, womanish scream, but the Choctaw calmly ignored him, wiping the blade clean on Baxter's pants leg.

"You say it was self-defense, Fargo?" Jeffries repeated. "Square deal?"

In the narrowest sense, Fargo knew it wasn't. Cranky Man had made the first move toward a weapon. But if he admitted that, the Choctaw would never leave town alive.

"Square deal," Fargo repeated. "I don't even know these men."

"Well, I do, which makes it easy to believe you. Besides, I couldn't see it good from across the street, which makes it your word against theirs. At least you haven't killed anybody yet—have you?"

Fargo shook his head. "I'm trying hard not to."

"Well, evidently you've had a busy day," the sheriff said. "The Sloan brothers and their cousin came to see me today. Claimed you shot their shack all to hell early this morning."

"Did they also tell you they ambushed me, Jessie, and Cranky Man outside of town this afternoon?"

"Did you see their faces?"

"Did they see mine this morning?" Fargo countered.

The sheriff sighed in frustration. "Said they did, but their word ain't worth a busted trace chain. Well, as usual with you, Fargo, I guess it's no harm, no foul. Maybe I should arrest you, though, just to remove the amount of lead in the air."

"If you do, I'll have to cooperate. But I'd take it kindly if you don't."

"To hell with kindness—it's just that, whoever you're working for, I suspect it's the right side. Besides, it'll take more than some yahoo's claim for me to arrest anybody, so at least keep your . . . adventures discreet. Although I got a feeling you won't."

Jeffries looked at the wounded men. "Well, guess I best borrow one of Dolomite's buckboards and get these two reprobates over to Doc Anslowe's. Fargo?"

"Yeah?"

"You're a likable enough cuss, but trouble seems to follow you like a loyal mutt. Any chance you'll be moving on soon?"

Yet again, Fargo noticed, the sheriff wasn't asking him any details about why he was in town and creating all this ruckus. That seemed a logical question for a town sheriff to ask. Either someone had told him or he'd guessed.

"As soon as I can," Fargo promised.

Jeffries nodded. "That wasn't a warning, by the way, just a question."

He looked at Cranky Man. "I know you speak English. It's legal for Indians to carry small knives on the reservation, but not off. I'm already taking a chance by not arresting you for jumping the rez, especially if you stay in town much longer. I can't guarantee your safety once word gets out you stabbed a white man."

"Even a cockroach like this one?"

"Eat shit, blanket ass!" Baxter managed. "You're carrion bait, hear me? *Both* of you!"

"See what I mean?" Jeffries said. "Give me a hand, you two."

Fargo and Cranky Man helped Jeffries hitch a team and load the two hard tails into a buckboard.

"Sure seems like he's doing his damndest to keep both of us out of jail," Cranky Man said as the buckboard rattled out of the yard.

"You and me have hitched our thoughts to the same tie-rail," Fargo agreed. "But why is he coddling us?"

"Can't just be my good looks. You said that pony soldier—Colonel Mackenzie—likes Jeffries. Maybe he told Jeffries why we're here."

Fargo nodded. "That could explain it. Or maybe we're more useful to him if we're not jugged. It's hard to hang a new crime on a man who's already locked up. Tell me, you ever meet a sheriff as easygoing as Jeffries?"

"The one up in Lead Hill, what's-his-name?"

"Hollis Maitland."

"Yeah, him. He wasn't much for ironfisted law."

Fargo nodded. "And if you recall, he was crooked as cat shit."

At the first thunk of a fist on his door, Fargo came fully awake. He reached down beside the bed and unlimbered his Colt, thumb-cocking it.

"Christ sakes, don't shoot through the door, Fargo," Cody Jeffries's voice pleaded with him. "I'm here on official business."

With the window boarded up except for a slit, it was hard for Fargo to gauge the time. The bright line between boards told him morning was well advanced.

"You finally arresting me?" he greeted Sheriff Jeffries, opening the door.

Jeffries slapped a packet of papers into Fargo's hand and stepped inside. "Damn, it's stuffy in here—and dark as the inside of a boot. Mind if I light some candles?"

"Knock yourself out. The hell is this?"

"A summons to appear in court this Saturday—that's tomorrow—at ten a.m. In other words, just go downstairs—we hold court in the saloon."

By now there was enough light for Fargo to peruse the papers. His face grew more and more incredulous. "Well, I'll be hung for a horse thief . . ."

"It don't go quite *that* far," Jeffries said, setting his solid bulk onto the chair. "This is what you call a tort—a redress for supposed wrongs that don't involve criminal charges."

"Baxter Sanford and Jonas Wheeling, plaintiffs," Fargo read from the neatly written, but bombastic page. "How could those two chawbacons rig this up so fast?"

"Long story short, that needle-dick bug-humper J. C. McGrady saw me haul them to Doc Anslowe's office last night. He got them plastered with a bottle of red-eye, and this is the result."

"This says they want my horse plus five-hundred dollars for damages and—and *lost wages*? You telling me those puke pails work?"

"According to McGrady, they're trappers."

"Yeah, and I'm the Prince of Wales. Says here Jonas wants my horse as 'sufficient recompense for movable goods caused to be ruined by Skye Fargo's aggravated battery upon the person of one Jonas Wheeling.' Jesus H. Christ! McGrady musta piled this on with a shovel. It's English, but I can't make sense of it."

"McGrady claims Jonas had a valuable horse tethered in graze outside of town. Also claims a wolf pack killed it because Jonas couldn't get back to it in time after you knocked him sick and silly. I'm going to check into it later."

"So you're saying this . . . summons is legal?"

"It's sheep dip, but it's legal. I hope you mean to show up?"

"I always obey the law when I can't avoid it. So you're telling me Pine Hollow has a judge?"

"He's the township magistrate, actually. A circuit rider who comes here once a month, and tomorrow happens to be the day. Folks just call him 'Judge' as a courtesy. Name's Otis Breedlove, a former Texas Ranger who lost his left arm to a Comanche war axe."

"So that's why McGrady slapped this together so quick," Fargo said. "Will there be a jury?"

Jeffries shook his head. "A magistrate don't preside over jury trials. Otis will render the final verdict."

"What about Cranky Man? Is he in the mix?"

"Nope, the law says he can't be. Indians are considered heathens, which means they can't be held to the phrase, 'So help me God.' Even if he was Christian, all rez Indians are federal wards and can't be tried in local courts."

"But Baxter and Jonas," Fargo put in with biting sarcasm, "will tell the truth and nothing but the truth, so help them God."

"Are you kidding? Those two would sell the baby Jesus to Comancheros."

"I wonder if I need a lawyer," Fargo mused aloud.

Sheriff Jeffries pushed to his feet and headed toward the door. "Good hunting on that one. We only got one so-called lawyer in this area, and that's McGrady. Even in Arkansas a lawyer can't represent both sides in the same case, or he would."

Fargo speared his fingers through his hair. "Ain't *this* the drizzlin' shits?"

"Well, I've got fish to fry," Jeffries said, letting himself out. In the hallway he turned to look at Fargo. "Trial's tomorrow, ten a.m. And, Fargo, don't fret this foolishness. Judge Breedlove is a down-to-earth frontiersman who's got no patience with these cheapjack lawyers."

"I hope so," Fargo said, "because *any* man who tries to take my stallion is gonna wish he'd died as a child."

The moment Fargo reached the bottom of the stairs, he knew it was time for a showdown.

The flashy sharper in the brocade vest was the only man in the saloon besides Dave. He sat at his usual table, riffling a deck of cards and waiting to hook a fish.

"Morning, sport," he called to Fargo. "Still too busy to face your Waterloo?"

"Well, I reckon comes a time a man's got to fight or show yellow, huh?"

"I'll be gentle with you."

Fargo crossed to the bar and planked four Liberty head gold eagles, the last of his pay from the Nebraska Territory job.

"Morning, Dave. Give me forty dollars in chips."

"Watch that fucker," Dave warned. "He pulls in business, but he's a sleight-of-hand artist. I'm surprised he hasn't been shot by now."

Fargo joined the sharper and spilled his chips out onto the green baize surface of the table.

"Forty dollars! That's pin money. You have to bet big to win big, stout lad."

Fargo took a seat facing him. "Look, why don't you forget all this 'sport' and 'chappie' and 'stout lad' foolishness? My name's Skye Fargo. Just call me Fargo. What's yours?"

"Daniels. Gilbert Daniels."

"Good, solid name. All right, here you go, Daniels."

Fargo set ten dollars in chips aside, sliding them over to his adversary. "This is for you."

Daniels's brow wrinkled under a huge stack of pomaded hair. "What for?"

"I never clean a man out at cards. I always leave him burying money."

The unexpected words struck Daniels like a slap to the face. "How did killing come into this?"

"Don't take me wrong. I've never killed a man for cheating at cards. I figure someone else will do it, anyway, and why have it on my conscience? But the way you been fleecing the rubes in this town, I doubt you'll make it out alive."

Daniels chuckled. "I pegged you all wrong, Fargo. I figured a man wearing bloody buckskins must be a hick."

"Quite a few have made that mistake. All right, let's get down to brass tacks. First standing rule: no peeking at the deadwood."

"That's my rule, too."

"Next standing rule," Fargo said, "stud poker, no wild cards."

"Better and better. A man's game."

"Last rule: we play only ten hands, table stakes, no bets beyond the money showing. I got no use for IOUs."

Daniels flashed his wire-tight smile. "I won't need ten hands to clean out thirty dollars at table stakes."

"Newcomer deals," Fargo said, scooping up the deck. He noticed Daniels was sporting some new artillery, a pair of fancy Remingtons with ivory grips. "Becoming a two-gun curly wolf, are you?"

"After that crack you made about a hideout gun, I figured I'd wear my weapons in the open."

Fargo dealt the hand. A quick round of betting brought the pot up to twenty dollars.

"I'll take two," Daniels said.

"And the dealer stands pat."

A final round of betting brought the pot up to forty dollars.

Daniels slapped down his hand. "Read 'em and weep. Full house, aces over jacks."

He started to scoop the chips in, but Fargo caught his wrist. "Read 'em and choke. Royal flush."

Daniels turned brick red and scooted his chair back. His hands slid toward the edge of the table. "Maybe I'm about to draw a pair of sixes."

Fargo laughed, and an eyeblink later his Colt was leveled on the sharper. "Sorry. One of a kind beats a pair in *draw* poker."

"Fargo, don't kill him in here!" Dave begged from up front. "I got a weak stomach for cleaning up brains."

Daniels went from mad to astonished in a heartbeat. "Katy Christ, you are quicker than I thought, Fargo. Is that holster of yours spring-loaded?"

Fargo sheathed his gun. "Now there's an idea. Tell me the truth—how long you been waiting to use that 'pair of sixes' line?"

Daniels looked sheepish. "Since I bought the shooters, but I wasn't stupid enough to draw on you. But, say ... how in the hell could you draw a royal flush and not even discard?"

"The same way you can produce three aces after I pulled two from the deck."

Fargo pulled the two aces in question from his sleeve and dropped them onto the table.

"So you're admitting you cheated?"

"I'm admitting *we* cheated," Fargo corrected him. "I told you I'd whip you on your own terms."

Both men stared at each other for perhaps ten seconds, then burst out laughing simultaneously.

"That just flat does it for me," Daniels admitted. "From now on I play an honest game. Fargo, where did you learn to sharp like that?"

"Riverboats, mostly between Cincinnati and New Orleans. Those are some wide-open games, and if you can't cheat you can't play."

Daniels looked around to make sure nobody was listening. "I read somewhere that it was foolish pride that created the devil, not evil. I apologize for acting like a damn fool these past few days. It's embarrassing to admit this, Fargo, but I can't stand it when I see a better man than me—makes me have to show him up."

"That's foolish, all right. The only man you have to best is the one who braces you. Besides, you look like a fellow who can give a good accounting of himself."

"Well, fighting is one thing, women another. I've had women up and leave me on the spot for rugged men like you."

"Women? So that's what it's all about?" Fargo chuckled. "Way I see it, they're here for our pleasure. If one leaves, just tell her to leave the door open for the next one."

Fargo paused, studying Daniels's suddenly lovesick face. "That mustache of yours is glued on, isn't it?"

"Yep. And these wrinkles around my eyes—I get them from going to bed with a brine-soaked cloth tied around my eyes. I'm only nineteen."

All at once Fargo understood. "Christ. *That's* why you're in here every night. Gilbert, you've fallen hard for Felicity Meadows, right?"

"I'd kiss the devil's ass in hell if she asked me to. Please don't noise it around, or I'll have to leave town. I'll bet she's under your spell by now, right? Just like that pretty Jessie Ravenel?"

"Felicity hates my guts," Fargo assured him, which he didn't altogether believe. "But it doesn't matter a jackstraw because I'm in love with women, not woman."

"You, I could understand her falling for. But what does she see in that big, bull-necked sheriff? He ain't a bad sort, but he's too coarse and homely for her."

Fargo alerted like a hound on point. "Cody Jeffries? So you think she's the sheriff's fancy-piece?"

"I don't think it, I *know* it. They're making the two-backed beast almost every day. I've followed her to his house and listened outside the bedroom window—you can't mistake those sounds. *What* does she see in him?"

"I wonder," Fargo said. "No accounting for taste, I reckon."

But Felicity's own words, spoken yesterday in front of her

hotel, now burned in Fargo's mind like embers: *It's a man's bank account that matters to me.*

Fargo's boot heels thumped along the boardwalk as he headed toward the livery, his eyes in shadow under the wide brim of his hat. Besides his known enemies, he now had to worry about vigilantes and reward seekers looking to pop him over, so his right hand rested lightly on his holster, ready to pull steel.

He spotted Jimmy Parker, the spunky kid who'd saved his life on Fargo's first day in town. The boy was peeling an apple with a pocketknife outside Chandler's Mercantile.

"Hey, hero!" Fargo greeted him.

The kid flushed with pleasure. "Aww . . . say, Mr. Fargo! Is it true you gotta go to court tomorrow?"

Fargo winced. "It's all over town, is it?"

"Sure. I seen it in the broadsheet on the dance hall wall. Everybody's gonna be there." He suddenly scowled. "Well, everybody 'cept women and kids. They ain't allowed. Pa says—"

"James Elmore Parker, you get in here right this minute!"

A stern-faced woman wearing a starched bonnet stepped outside. She gave Fargo the evil eye, then grabbed Jimmy by one arm and jerked him inside the store. As Fargo passed the open doorway he heard her scolding words:

"—man is criminal riffraff, a murderer and thief. You stay *far* away from the likes of him."

"But, Ma, Mr. Fargo is my friend. He—"

The sound of a resounding slap ended the conversation in favor of the biddy. Fargo had seen increasing signs he was being "cut" by the entire town. It was a worrisome portent since he would soon be going before a magistrate.

He found Dolomite pounding caulks into old horseshoes and Cranky Man asleep in the loft. Even before Fargo cleared the ladder, however, the Choctaw bolted awake, leveling the Dragoon on him.

"You're lucky I'm sober, hair face, or your guts would be dangling off the rafters."

"Guess you haven't heard yet I'm being taken to court?"

Cranky Man groped for his hip flask. "Guess again. Dolomite woke me up and told me this morning. So them two scum buckets want your horse?"

"And five hundred dollars."

"You worried?"

"Well, feelings are running pretty strong against me in this town. So if it goes bad tomorrow, I want you ready for a hot bust out. Horses tacked, all your weapons loaded. I don't give a damn about Colonel Mackenzie's problems—I'll hightail it to the Snake River country until this blows over. My stallion won't become an outlaw's horse."

"Dolomite tells me that Baxter and Jonas got no friends in Pine Hollow. And the judge was a Texas Ranger. Dolomite thinks maybe you'll win."

Fargo nodded. "Sheriff seems to think so, too. In that case, me and you get a wiggle on and expose this holdup ring fast before we get boosted branchward by vigilantes. I got some ideas, but I still need proof."

The Trailsman had just started back down the ladder when Cranky Man said, "Fargo?"

"Yeah?"

"I took this job with you for the money. Hell, why should a reservation buck care a frog's fat ass what happens to whiteskin pony soldiers? But I keep seeing them soldiers, and them two on the pay wagon, cut down in cold blood. It . . . ah, I ain't one for words."

"I take your drift, old son. It's eating at me, too."

"You know, I like Sheriff Jeffries. You think he's mixed up in this holdup ring?"

"I like him, too, but I don't know what to think just yet. I'll tell you this much, though—if we prove he *is* in on the heists, he'll get no mercy from me."

Fargo next retraced his steps along Main Street, heading for the bathhouse behind the hotel. The proprietor was an elderly Chinese man wearing the floppy blue blouse of the working class. Fargo paid him four bits, and the old gent handed him a coarse towel and a lump of yellowish lye-and-tallow soap.

He pointed to a fire pit with large buckets of water heating on metal slats. "You go stall number seven. Boy bring water."

The bathhouse was divided into two halves, one for each sex. Fargo found a tiny, private stall with a wooden tub and two hooks on the wall for clothing and gun belts. A doltish-looking kid with a huge goiter filled the tub with steaming water. Fargo stripped from hat to boots and took his Colt with him into the tub, gasping at the heat.

The curtain shielding his stall rippled, and Fargo swung his short gun over, finger curled around the trigger.

"Don't shoot, long-tall. You'll have another charge to answer in court."

Lynette, wearing a figure-flattering anchor-print dress, slipped in to join him. Her pale blond hair was a mass of ringlets.

"Jesus God, woman, at least pre-*tend* you got more brains than a rabbit. I was a cat whisker away from plugging you."

"I wish you *would* 'plug' me, but since you refuse, I'm at least gonna give you a bath."

"Look, I can do that myself. I don't trust—"

"Shush it," she ordered him, grabbing the soap and sudsing his chest and armpits. "Good God a-gorry, look at them scars on you! And that hard chest. Soon we'll have you slick and shiny as a new saddle."

Her ministrations were effective and relaxing. Fargo knew he should chase the scheming little wretch out, but he was literally in her hands now and helpless to stop her.

"Now," she said a minute later, "let's get to your man parts."

She plunged her hand into the soapy water. "Whoa! I see *this* boy's feeling sparky! Now, that's a pizzle to feel proud of, and I oughta know."

Fargo tried to balance conflicting impulses of safety and pleasure, but she had decided the issue for him when she took him in hand. Her soap-slick fingers moved faster, squeezed harder, shooting hot, tickling currents of intense pleasure down his shaft and into his groin.

"Lord, he's really angry now," Lynette said, pumping faster and harder. "He's coming out of the water after me. Let's calm him down before he destroys the town."

Fargo's breathing quickened and grew raspy as the welling pressure made his whole body twitch. The Colt clattered to the floor when he lost control of his muscles just before exploding in release. A dazed lassitude crept over him while Lynette finished scrubbing his body.

There was a low, small window in the west wall to let steam escape. Fargo heard hoof clops and then spotted Felicity Meadows on her chestnut mare, riding out of town. Going to meet

Cody Jeffries, according to the lovesick young gambler in the Razorback, and Fargo believed it. But what else should he believe about those two?

Lynette saw him gazing out the window. "Now ain't *she* high-toned? 'Course, she ain't a whore—not much, I reckon."

"Where is she headed?" Fargo asked, curious to know if Gilbert Daniels had shared his secret.

"Straight to hell, for aught I care, the stuck-up bitch. Talk is, she's diddling some rich old duffer. There's several live around here. She's selling her muff just like me, only she don't split the money with Dave."

Fargo gave her a teasing grin. "Is that any way to talk about your employer?"

She slapped his shoulder. "You and your paid-spy foolishness! I'd eat dog turds before I'd do her bidding. Can't a gal just have a case on you?"

"I have no evidence you're a spy," Fargo admitted.

"I'm your friend, Skye Fargo. I can prove it in court tomorrow if you call me as a witness."

Fargo watched her from speculative eyes. "How?"

"Jonas Wheeling claims he's stove up bad from you beatin' on him, right?"

"Yeah. So?"

"He's put the word out how you ruint his back. So just call me as a witness, that's all."

Fargo's lips twitched into a grin as he caught on. "Well, I just might do that."

10

On the afternoon of Skye Fargo's fourth day in northeast Arkansas, the five malefactors on his list met in the same shack Fargo had riddled with bullets. Butch Sloan, his florid face even redder with angry frustration at his peers, kept a wary eye out the open door as he addressed the others.

"Boys, this is no time to go puny. It's been confirmed by our source that there's a shipment coming from the supply depot at Little River to the outpost at Booneville, east of us. Blankets, rations, liquor, coffee, sugar, ammo . . . I got a buyer up in Saint Joe who outfits pilgrims for the Oregon Trail. After we kill the express rider and the military escort, he'll be waiting with two freight wagons to load it up. Two thousand simoleans in pure gold. We can hit it tomorrow in good ambush country."

Baxter Sanford, still pale from blood loss the day before, slowly shook his head. "I don't rightly know, Butch. I mean, could be we're going once too often to the well. It was only last Tuesday we hit the pay wagon. And Fargo—"

"Fargo! That's the beauty of it, Bax. We strike tomorrow while he's trapped in court."

"We? Christ, Jonas and me gotta be in court, too."

"So? You and Jonas ain't up to full fighting fettle, anyhow. This bullshit lawsuit worked up by McGrady is perfect. It keeps Fargo on a short tether. I hired a couple reliable guns from Van Buren to fill in for you two, but you'll get your share. Plus extra for Jonas to buy him a new horse."

Scout Langley, squatting on his heels against the back wall, pushed the curled brim of his hat back to see his cousin better.

"Baxter's right," he said, voice flattened of emotion. "Two jobs in one week is paring the cheese mighty close to the rind. I say we kill Fargo before we do anything else."

"Nix on the calamity howling. I all the time hear how Fargo is hell on two sticks. But what's he done so far 'cept keep himself alive? I tell you, he's overrated."

"Sure he is," Baxter shot back. "And every Jack will have his Jill, too. Put that claptrap away from your mind right now, Butch. The road to hell is paved with the bones of men who underrated Fargo."

"Hell, what has the son of a bitch done? Name it."

"He's getting his ducks all in a row, that's what, and when he makes his big move, we'll know it. My stick floats the same way as Scout's—kill Fargo first."

"Scout, huh?" Butch said, casting a dubious glance at his cousin. "Big scout, my ass. Scout said he wouldn't lay down a trail, that night he bollixed the explosion. But Fargo showed up here just hours after."

"He didn't need a trail," Scout objected. "After you and Romer made asses of yourself in the saloon, he knew it was us. All he had to do was ask where we live."

Butch ignored him, pointing to the east wall. "Look, boys, Fargo shot it to a sieve. And this was after Scout made his brag he'd kill Fargo on that first day the bastard come to town. Claimed he never missed with a knife to the back."

Scout's furtive, consumption-glazed eyes snapped with anger. "It was that damn snot-nosed brat that warned him. And what about you, big man? You woke up yesterday morning vowing we'd all shoot Fargo and that blanket ass to wolf bait. We blasted over two hundred cartridges and didn't even crease either one of them."

Butch waved this off. "Ah, he just rolled a seven, that's all."

"A man cheats death four times in a row," Baxter said, "and it's just luck?"

Butch's tone grew more cajoling. "Boys, you're takin' your eyes off the bead. We only got two more heists before we shut down this operation and go our separate ways, rich men. One's tomorrow, when we'll know where Fargo is. The other's that bullion coach passing near here on its way to New Orleans, and I need the five of us for that last one—no hired replacements, just experienced hands. This is no time for backing and filling— just *two* more, and we'll all be sitting in the catbird seat."

"We ain't even suspects so far," Romer pitched in to help

his brother. "Remember, we got bulletproof alibis for the past robberies. That's more than Fargo can say."

"He'll have a damn good one tomorrow," Baxter pointed out.

"So what?" Butch retorted. "He sat one out, is all. Christ sakes, to hear you and Scout take on about it, we're wearing hemp neckties already. I admit Fargo worries me some, but he's the only fly in the ointment."

"Sure," Scout spoke up. "But Jonas and Baxter found out he's a mighty big fly. Butch, the job tomorrow is all right, but I'd think long and hard about this bullion coach until we know Fargo is planted."

"Get off my dick! You don't destroy the lawn to kill the crabgrass."

"We'll fix Fargo's flint," Romer chipped in. "He's gun-handy and shiftier than a creased buck, but we'll geld him. He's out of the way tomorrow, so it's hawg-stupid not to heist them supplies. Then we either kill Fargo or pin the blame on him."

Everyone nodded at the logic of that, and Butch calmed down. He perched on the corner of a trestle table, took out the makings, and built a cigarette, pinching the end of the quirly and twisting it. He scratched a phosphor to life on the table and lit his smoke.

"Jonas!" he called out. "You ain't said nothing. The hell's got into you, religion?"

"I ain't in no whistlin' mood, is all."

"'Course you ain't. Takes teeth to whistle proper, and Fargo knocked yours out. But these days you can afford them walrus-ivory choppers they make in Saint Louis."

"He's still sulking over that blood bay of his that got killed by wolves," Baxter supplied. "Iffen he'd left it with the rest of our horses—"

"I told you the bay had two loose shoes, and I didn't have no shoeing hammer," Jonas cut him off. "I was planning to take her to the blacksmith in Overton."

"A by-God man don't ride a mare, anyhow," Butch scoffed. "Maybe we got a gal-boy here, fellows."

The others laughed.

"This bullion coach," Jonas said just to change the subject. "You think it's a good idea, us planning the job ourself?"

"Listen, mooncalf, does your mother know you're out? Why should *we* get the crappy end of the stick? So far, we take all the risks, and the big bug collects half the loot for just sittin' on his pratt. So he got cold feet on this last one and pulled out—that just means we don't got to split it with nobody. It's gravy, and all for us."

Butch paused to give his next words weight. "As for Fargo—tomorrow he's right where we want him. But framing him for the holdups will be our second choice. By the time that bullion coach rolls past, we want him cold as a cellar floor."

It was a ludicrously solemn procession passing through the propped-open batwings of the Razorback Saloon: Baxter Sanford, a crutch propped under his left arm; Jonas Wheeling on a stretcher made from a horse blanket and rake handles, two town loafers lugging him; and finally, J. C. McGrady wearing white flannel trousers, a black wool frockcoat, and a foppish powdered wig.

The saloon was packed—standing room only—and erupted in laughter and catcalls. Fargo, seated at the defendant's table, enjoyed a chuckle at the comedic spectacle.

"Blamed fool," he muttered, looking at McGrady's ill-fitting wig. The self-proclaimed lawyer looked as if Indians had scalped him, then thrown it carelessly back on.

The place was still in an uproar when Judge Otis Breedlove, the empty left arm of his coat neatly pinned up, stepped inside. Fargo knew this frontier type at a glance: a gruff old coot, unpolished but savvy, strict, earthy, informal. If a face could have a motto, his would be: *Nothing ruins truth like stretching it.*

"Order!" he commanded. "Order in the court! This ain't a damn Bowery show! What the consarn?" he added, spotting McGrady's wig. "Is your head cold, Mr. McGrady?"

"No, your honor. I am a traditionalist."

A table—on which sat a Bible, a revolver, and a pitcher of water—and a horsehair chair had been placed at the front of the saloon for Breedlove.

"For your information," he told McGrady as he sat down, "we whipped the British and sent them packing a long time ago. But wear that asinine wig if you like—unless it draws nesting birds.

"All right, gentlemen," he called out, "we're assembled here today to—"

Breedlove halted, and Fargo realized he had spotted Lynette standing by the staircase.

"Beg pardon, ma'am," he told her. "No women or kids allowed."

Fargo stood up. "Judge, I'm Skye Fargo, the, ah, defendant in this case. I'm hoping to call Miss Lynette Berman as a witness."

Breedlove took Fargo's measure in a probing glance. "All right, Mr. Fargo, so long as it's not just a sideshow. As I was saying, the case before us today is a tort in which plaintiffs, Jonas Wheeling and Baxter Sanford, seek redress from Skye Fargo for alleged personal and property injuries. Mr. McGrady, make your opening statement, but I warn you: lawyering the truth ain't the same as telling it. Skip the twaddle and bunkum and give the pertinent information."

"Yes, your honor. Plaintiffs intend to prove that on Thursday evening, the twenty-fifth of May extant, they stopped by Dolomite Jones's livery stable to water their horses. Because it was dark, they did not see Mr. Fargo and a Choctaw Indian accomplice lurking in the shadows to rob them."

"Sure!" shouted Jake Ravenel's voice from the crowd. "And oysters can walk upstairs, too, you lying pup!"

Breedlove brought his gavel down. "Order! I'll not tolerate such outbursts. At the moment this is a court of law, not a saloon. Proceed, Mr. McGrady."

"The Indian threw a knife at Baxter Sanford, causing a severe injury that will be described by Dr. Anslowe. Fargo, meantime, pulled Jonas Wheeling hard from the saddle, seriously injuring Wheeling's back. When Mr. Wheeling fell to his knees, helpless, Mr. Fargo brutally brought his knee up into Wheeling's face, causing the loss of six teeth. Only the arrival of Sheriff Jeffries prevented the subsequent robbery and murder of my clients."

McGrady made a great show of gazing into the eyes of his audience, presenting the very picture of moral rectitude. Besides the Ravenel boys, Fargo spotted Sheriff Jeffries, café owner Tubby Blackford, the saloon keeper, Dave, and the lovesick card sharper, Gilbert Daniels. But Fargo abruptly realized the Sloan brothers and their cousin were not in the gathering. Why would they miss the possible skewering of the Trailsman?

"But the gravest loss," McGrady droned on, "was suffered

by Jonas Wheeling. He had tethered a magnificent dapple gray horse just outside of town, intending to retrieve it after enjoying a drink or two at the Razorback. But as you can see, the attack by Mr. Fargo left my client incapable of returning. And during the night, this horse was torn apart by a pack of wolves."

McGrady gave his talk a pulpit pause, building the drama. "No doubt most of the men assembled here now have heard the ominous reports about Skye Fargo—"

"McGrady, pack it in. You know damn good and well," Breedlove cut him off, "that accusations and rumors can't be brought up in court, only prior convictions. Skip the rumors and stick to the facts."

"Very well, your honor." McGrady opened his arms in a rhetorical flourish. "That, your honor, is a précis of our case, every syllable the sacred truth."

Just as McGrady fell silent, a manure wagon rattled by in the street, clearly visible through the open doors. Its pungent odor wafted into the saloon.

"*There's* your précis!" someone roared out in a voice that shook the studding, and laughter exploded.

Breedlove gaveled the audience back to order, but was too busy laughing himself to issue any warning.

"Mr. Fargo, do you have any opening statement?"

Fargo stood up. "Well, Judge, just that almost everything McGrady said is a pack of lies. Him and his ilk are writing the frontier's epitaph. He knows those two graveyard rats he calls 'clients' are so low they could walk under a snake's belly on stilts. So let's get thrashing—I'll prove the whole bunch are lily-livered liars."

"Kiss my white ass, buckskin boy," Baxter snarled.

Breedlove banged his gavel. "You're out of order, Sanford. One more word out of your filthy sewer, and I'll have you arrested for contempt of court. And you, Wheeling, wipe that smug smirk off your map. That stretcher don't fool me."

"Oh, but, your honor," McGrady blandished like a rented toady, "a back injury—"

"Since Mr. Fargo," Breedlove cut him off impatiently, "lacks counsel, I'll intervene on his behalf as I see fit." He stared at Baxter and Jonas and added, "Neither one of you ugly buzzards amounts up to much in my opinion. But I'll set that aside and judge only the merits of your case. Likewise, Mr. Fargo, with your storied feats and considerable reputation. Call your first witness, Mr. McGrady."

"Call Skye Fargo."

Breedlove swore him in, and Fargo sat in the witness chair. McGrady assumed a smug smile, playing to the audience. "Now, Mr. Fargo, since you are a known Indian lover—"

"Badgering the witness," Breedlove snapped. "And prejudicial language."

"Ahem. Mr. Fargo, since it is a known fact that you are accompanied by a Choctaw Indian, does the Christian oath you just took mean anything to you?"

"McGrady," Breedlove said in an ominous tone, "why are you playing to a jury that isn't here? These people aren't voting, so quit the stumping. We want none of the parsley and all of the meat."

McGrady's red, bulbous nose twitched. "As you wish. Just a few questions to show what manner of man we're dealing with. Mr. Fargo, would you say you've killed many men in your lifetime?"

"More than I can remember," Fargo said cheerfully. "And every one of them required killing."

"Indeed? And you can boast of it openly?"

"Why not? You've got the guts to wear that stupid wig."

"Gentlemen," Breedlove said when the laughter subsided, "avoid this clash of stags."

McGrady said, "Would you also say that you've created plenty of enemies?"

"Sure. There's plenty who hope to see me dance on air or die in the dirt."

"Are you prepared to tell this court *why* you're in Pine Hollow?"

"Nope," Fargo said, leaving it there.

"Damn it, McGrady," Judge Breedlove interrupted, "we have freedom of movement in America. Mr. Fargo doesn't have to tell us why he's here unless you can prove its relevance. Stick to the case at hand."

McGrady clasped his hands behind his back and paced back and forth with his chin tucked in. Suddenly he nearly shouted, "Acknowledge the corn, Mr. Fargo! You and your redskin accomplice did not act in self-defense—you brutally attacked my clients, intending to kill and rob them. Only the sheriff's arrival stopped you."

"Well, you're right on one point," Fargo conceded. "If we hadn't noticed the sheriff coming, we'd likely have killed them—and earned jewels in paradise for doing it. But you're wrong about the robbery part, and we didn't start the fandango, they did. As for this 'brutal' foolishness—there was nothing brutal about it. Once a man slaps for his shooter, you want me to powder his butt and tuck him in?"

McGrady puckered his brow in disgust. "Call Baxter Sanford."

Breedlove swore him in and Sanford took the witness chair, putting on quite a show with the crutch. Under questioning by his lawyer, he told the same story as in the opening statement.

"Are you certain," McGrady asked at one point, "that neither you nor Jonas Wheeling reached for your guns first?"

"Sure as the Lord made Moses."

When it was Fargo's turn to cross-examine, he said, "Sanford, you claim it was the Choctaw who knifed you?"

"Hell, you know it was. You was right there."

"Did *I* lay a hand on you?"

"Object! Incompetent, irrelevant, and immaterial," McGrady protested. His face turned desperate as he realized where this was going. "I did not raise the issue, during examination, of Fargo attacking Baxter."

"Overruled," Breedlove said. "Physical attacks are at the heart of this trial. Answer the question, Sanford."

"I'll tell the world you never laid a hand on me," Baxter boasted to Fargo's face, "or you'd a been wearin' your ass for a hat."

Breedlove chuckled. "Well played, Fargo," he muttered. Out loud he said, "The court summarily dismisses Baxter Sanford from this case because he has no standing in this court. His beef is with the Choctaw Nation, not Fargo, since Indians can't be duly sworn in white courts. Call your next witness, Mr. McGrady."

McGrady, his face a sickly green, said, "Call Jonas Wheeling. Your honor, because my client—"

"Yes, he can testify from where he is," Breedlove said. "Testifying from a 'stretcher' seems quite appropriate for this client."

Wheeling, too, obviously well coached, repeated the same story that Sanford had told.

"I paid two hunnert dollars for that horse," he wound up his testimony. "Best horse I ever owned. And when Baxter told me she was et by wolves, it just kicked the guts right outta me."

She. Hearing that telltale word, Fargo slid forward in his chair. But he held his powder for now and asked no questions of Wheeling.

Next McGrady called Dr. Jeremy Anslowe, who described the injuries suffered by both men.

"And did they tell you, Doctor, how they received those injuries?" McGrady asked.

"Don't answer that, Doc," Breedlove intervened. "Since you weren't at the livery during the fracas, it's only hearsay. Doc, I'm curious. Did Jonas Wheeling *walk* in and out of your office?"

"Well, he was out pretty good when the sheriff brought him, and the two of us carried him in. I let him rest on a cot in the office and I went to bed, so I don't know how he left."

"Did he complain about his back?"

"No, but I gave him a good dose of laudanum, and he went to sleep quick."

"Judge," Fargo spoke up, deciding to play an ace, "maybe I'm out of turn here, but could I call Miss Lynette Berman to testify on this point?"

"Order of the witnesses is at the court's discretion," Breedlove replied. "The court calls Miss Berman."

"Object, your honor!" McGrady sputtered, shooting to his feet. "This woman has impeached her own credibility by virtue of her scandalous profession. No offense intended," he added as Lynette passed his table.

"Well, plenty taken," she shot back.

"Your honor," McGrady persisted, "this woman cannot be allowed to taint the sanctity—"

"Oh, botheration!" Lynette snapped, plopping into the witness chair. "You're a bigger whore than I am, McGrady. I screw a man for a dollar; you're trying to screw Mr. Fargo for all he's got and more, you low-down, spineless, needle-dick windbag— and believe me, it *is* a needle."

McGrady flushed scarlet while the saloon erupted in cheers and laughter. Breedlove was slow to gavel it back to order.

"Miss Berman," the judge said after swearing her in, taking over the questioning, "you are a . . . lady of the night?"

"Yessir. Night, mornings, afternoons—I'm a round-the-clock whore. And lots a fellers in this saloon right now will tell you I'm a huckleberry above a persimmon when it comes to—"

"We take your drift, Miss Berman," the judge cut her off. "Try to confine yourself to the questions at hand and avoid unrelated remarks. The issue before the court at this moment is the condition of Mr. Wheeling's back. Do you have something pertinent to say on that topic?"

"Yessir, I surely do. Skye Fargo is s'posed to have injured that back around sundown this past Thursday. But about two o'clock Friday morning Wheeling walked into my room. His mouth was all messed up, and there was fresh blood on his shirt. But any man who can poke a gal doggy style on his knees, then flip her around into the missionary without missing a beat has got the strong back of a mule."

"Judge, I object!" McGrady shouted above a roar of laughter. "This slattern is a calculated liar paid by Mr. Fargo!"

"Blow it out your bunghole," Lynette retorted.

"McGrady, if you can't prove that charge you just made," Breedlove warned, "it stands as a slander."

"Forgive me, Miss Berman. I spoke in the heat of anger, your honor. But my client's back injury is severe—he groans constantly."

"He was groaning yesterday morning, all right," Lynette said. "And toward the end he was howlin' like a dog in the hot moons. But he *wasn't* suffering no damn back pain. I worked him good."

"She's telling the straight, Judge," Dave called out. "I remember now that I sold Jonas a token just before closing time. His mouth was all swollen, but he was walking fine."

Breedlove stared at Wheeling, his face a mask of Old Testament wrath. "Mister, you've got a choice: stand up right now, or I charge you and your 'lawyer' with a fraud upon this court."

"Get the hell up!" McGrady said in a hoarse mutter, and a sheepish Jonas rose to his feet.

"Why, I do feel better," he said in a penitent tone.

"Mr. McGrady," Breedlove said, "you seem to have more conclusions than facts to warrant them. Baxter Sanford's claim has no standing, and Mr. Wheeling's back has miraculously healed. I'm inclined to dismiss the charges against Mr. Fargo."

"That would be hasty, your honor, and a miscarriage of justice. The loss of six teeth is a serious matter when a man only had twelve to start with, and there's Mr. Wheeling's valuable horse."

"Mr. Fargo cannot be held liable for the horse *or* the teeth," the magistrate reminded him, "unless you can provide a reliable witness to prove Fargo started the fight. And the sheriff's report on the incident assigns no blame—is that correct, Sheriff Jeffries?"

"That's the way of it, Judge," Cody Jeffries called out. "I didn't know there was any serious trouble until I heard Baxter bawling like a bay steer. It was one man's word against another's."

"Judge," Fargo put in, "I think it might bear fruit to poke into this horse business a little more. All right if I ask Jonas some questions along that line?"

"Since you're acting as your own counsel, that's your right."

Wheeling, however, had already realized his mistake and guessed where this might go. "Ah, let's forget about the horse, Fargo. It was McGrady pushed me into that. I'll just take the loss."

"Now hold on," Breedlove said, sniffing a rat. "Sheriff, did you actually confirm the death of this 'valuable' horse?"

"I took a look Thursday night, Judge, but clouds covered the moon and I found nothing. Then, yesterday, other duties kept me from looking."

Other duties . . . Fargo remembered watching Fel ride out of town.

"Judge," Fargo said, "I think we should take Jonas at his word on this one. He *did* lose a horse to wolves Thursday night, and a mighty fine horse, I'd wager. One nobody around town has likely seen. But I'd also wager it's not a dapple gray. Is it, Jonas?"

"Hell it ain't," Baxter piped up in support of his friend.

"Gelding or stallion, Jonas?"

"Why—a gelding."

"That's right, a gelding," Baxter affirmed.

Fargo grinned. "You two are piss-poor liars. I'd bet *my* horse the mount you lost is a mare. A blood-bay mare with a roached mane."

"Object," McGrady said weakly. "Argumentative and assuming facts not in evidence." But everyone, including his clients, ignored him.

Jonas shook his head stubbornly. "Fargo, I swear on the bones of my mother it ain't."

"Judge," Fargo said, "just a few minutes ago Jonas referred to the horse as 'she.'"

"That's right," Breedlove said. "But if there's a point to all this, Fargo, feel free to make it."

"All right. On Tuesday last I was a witness, through field glasses, to the latest payroll heist. I couldn't see the men real good—they were masked—but I studied the horses close. One was a blood bay with a roached mane. Later, I studied the ground where it stood when the outlaws broke open the strongbox. The horse had voided itself on the ground *behind* where it stood."

The saloon erupted in excited voices.

"That's a goddamn lie!" Jonas shouted.

"You better harken and heed," Breedlove warned him. "I'm on the verge of sending every man jack in this saloon out to beat the bushes. Wolves didn't eat enough to obscure that horse's coat or sex. If you force me to verify Fargo's claim, I'll double your prison stretch. Now, *out* with it man. Was it the horse Fargo described?"

"Well . . . all right, it was," Jonas confirmed, "but he's lying through his teeth about seeing that horse at the payroll heist. He seen her somewhere else and made it all up to frame me for his crime."

Fargo ignored this. "Nobody has seen this horse," Fargo added, "because the outlaws maintain separate mounts for their heists. Why else would Baron of Gray Matter here have to lie about the color and sex?"

"Now there's another lie! Nobody can prove I was in any robbery."

"That's correct for the time being," Breedlove said. "But evidently, Wheeling, you and your confederate are even stupider than God made you. You let this shyster trump up a phony case and you both perjure yourselves."

"Both?" Baxter protested. "It was *his* horse. Why you tryin' to fob it off on me?"

"You supported his lie. This court finds Jonas Wheeling and Baxter Sanford guilty of perjury. They are remanded over to the sheriff, who will hold them for sentencing at a later date. The case against Skye Fargo is dismissed."

By now both men were pouring sweat. Fargo winked at them. "It's the knot for sure, boys," he said in a low voice. "It's perjury that's putting you in jail, but it'll be robbery and murder by the time I'm done. Oh, it's the knot for sure."

11

After the surprise-ending trial in the Razorback, the citizens of Pine Bluff underwent a sea change in their attitude toward Skye Fargo.

There was still no definite proof that Sanford and Wheeling were members of the holdup gang, but Wheeling's confession about his "secret steed," as the latest broadsheet called it, left little doubt in the citizens' minds. The broadsheet also broadly hinted that Fargo must be in town to crack the gang, not lead it.

That belief only deepened when a telegram from the U.S. Army outpost at Booneville alerted Pine Bluff to the latest heist, one that very morning.

"Four troopers and two civilians sent under," Tubby Blackford reported while Fargo and Cranky Man tied into steaming plates of hash and grits. "I got it straight from the sheriff. The freighter was caught while climbing a steep grade surrounded by trees. The messenger rider got off only one round; the military guards were killed before they fired a shot."

"Any tracks reported?" Fargo asked.

"Five riders. Like always, they dispersed all over the compass. Two conveyances headed north, but that's saw-grass country and tracks don't last long."

When Tubby left to cook an order, Fargo remarked, "Well, that explains where Butch, Romer, and Scout were this morning. Operating on inside information."

"They musta hired on a couple more guns to replace Baxter and Jonas," Cranky Man speculated. "Plenty of 'em around."

Fargo nodded, his lips forming a grim, determined slit. "Six more dead men who might be alive if I'd've got the proof we need."

Cranky Man belched and pushed his plate away. "At least you got five names."

"Yeah, all the names except one—the topkick who's supplying information about the schedules and routes."

Cranky Man pulled out his sack of horehound drops and popped one into his mouth. "Now see, that's what I don't get. Why didn't this colonel give that information to you?"

"He can't by military law, and prob'ly wouldn't even if he could. Mackenzie has taken grief over my . . . methods in the past. That's why I'm just a bird dog for this one—it's not my job to stop these holdups. I'm just s'posed to look into 'em and try to identify the outlaws."

"So he can take the credit in the newspapers for capturing them," Cranky Man said. "Anyhow, the *outlaws* sure seem to know plenty."

"Yeah, don't they, though? That's where our topkick comes in. If we don't salt his tail, the five names on our list can just be switched out for new ones. The army can't stop these shipments, and they got no extra men for a large escort."

Fargo left six bits on the table, tossed a salute to Tubby, and went back outside into the glaring afternoon sunlight, Cranky Man following. Fargo took a careful look around.

"Lissenup," he told the Choctaw. "After that circus in the saloon today, the gang will be even more desperate to kill me— and you in the deal. I put heavy suspicion on Jonas and Baxter, and the rest are going to fear I've got the skinny on them, too."

"That rings right." Cranky Man's sullen face cracked in a rare smile. "Sounds like this whore Lynette is a game one. She pulled your bacon from the fire."

Fargo chuckled. "By God, she pitched into the game, all right. But I got a feeling Otis Breedlove had no plans to let those two vultures get my horse. Jonas was a damn fool—he had a hissy fit when he found out his mare was dead, and that even bigger fool McGrady talked him into going after my stallion."

Fargo fell silent, gaze sweeping the town as the two men headed back toward the livery. He felt hidden eyes on them, and a prickly tingling on his nape—a "God-fear" as many in this part of the country called it.

"Speaking of horses . . . it's not enough that we just suspect the Sloan brothers and Scout Langley. We need proof. The horses they keep just for holdups have to be in the area some-where, and we need to find them. I remember all the colors and markings from last Tuesday's heist. It could be a long search, so we'll set out early in the morning. Meantime . . ."

Fargo cast a glance toward the jailhouse. Cody Jeffries's buckskin was tied off out front.

"Tubby mentioned he'd be taking food over to the jail for Jeffries and the prisoners later," Fargo said. "The sheriff will have to stay with them since he's got no deputy."

"I take your drift," Cranky Man said. "We're gonna search his little love nest outside of town."

Fargo nodded. "The way you say. Let's face it: right now we're neither up the well nor down. We've got to stop tacking into the prevailing wind and chart our own course. And time is against us—who knows when the next strike is coming?"

"All that makes sense," Cranky Man agreed reluctantly. "But for a whiteskin, the sheriff seems like a decent sort. And a man's home . . ."

"Look, I hate like hell to do it. Jeffries could be innocent as a newborn. But if Gilbert Daniels is telling the truth, I now under-stand why the sheriff won't lock anybody up—that would keep him from meetings with Fel."

"Can you blame him? That's a fine-looking woman. Most men would give their left one just to sniff her garter."

"Far as her looks, she's right out of the top drawer," Fargo agreed. "But I can't see an upper-crust woman like her, one who talks like a book, staying in a burg like this just to sing in a sa-loon and play concubine for a homely sheriff—even if he *is* from a rich family, which we don't know for a fact. Something ain't quite jake there."

"The hell's a concubine?"

"A kept woman."

By now they'd reached the livery. Dolomite gave Fargo di-rections to Cody Jeffries's place. Both men tacked their horses and headed west out of town at a fast trot, eyes scouring all the potential ambush points.

Two miles outside of town Fargo spotted the low hill on the left that Dolomite had mentioned, and a thick line of willows screening the house behind.

"Well, cut off my legs and call me Shorty!" Cranky Man exclaimed in his mock Elijah Ravenel accent when they had ridden through the trees. "That's a mighty fancy wickiup."

The house was small but solidly built, with a veranda running along one side, gingerbread molding, and lancet-arched windows. Sunflowers grew shoulder high along the front.

"You'd never know it was here from the road," Fargo said, swinging down and hobbling the Ovaro. "We rode right past it coming into town."

In no time he found an unlocked bedroom window and both men crawled over the sill. They made a quick pass through the house to get their bearings and make sure no one was there.

"Man alive," Fargo said, "this place is furnished like a Kansas City gambling parlor."

He took in a big, claw-footed table of solid maple in the front parlor, carved-oak bookcases, heavy velvet draperies, and a Turkish rug with a knotted fringe.

"You know what stuff like this costs this far west?" he said. "Freighting charges alone would be a king's ransom."

"He *better* have a rich family," Cranky Man opined. "No way in hell could an honest badge-toter afford this layout."

"Pa Ravenel had a point when he said nobody knows for sure that Jeffries comes from wealth. Could be backcountry lore by now."

"If I take your drift," Cranky Man said, "you're saying that's a made-up story so Jeffries can openly spend his share of the holdup money?"

"I'm suggesting it, not saying it," Fargo corrected him as he rifled some desk drawers. "A crooked sheriff could be worth plenty to the gang. Especially for providing alibis and steering suspicion somewhere else."

"Like onto the Ravenels?"

Fargo nodded. "And he has other opportunities, besides these recent heists, to profit. Since a town sheriff is also the tax collector, it's easy to shave off some for himself. I even knew of a sheriff in the Kansas Territory who robbed banks in nearby towns."

"But if Jeffries is the topkick," Cranky Man said, "don't that mean he knows all the army plans for the shipments?"

"Likely, and that's a sticker. A local sheriff wouldn't be provided that information through routine channels. But soldiers draw low pay, and it ain't all that hard to bribe a company clerk. Anyhow, if Jeffries is in on it, he'll foul his nest before too long. C'mon."

The two men headed toward the bedroom at the rear of the house. The luxury was just as apparent here: a huge tester bed with satin sheets, a walnut highboy with ivory knobs, and a tall wardrobe with paneled doors. Fargo opened them up, then whistled sharply.

"Well, here's your chance to sniff that garter."

Cranky Man goggled at the contents. The female clothing including a sateen dress with black-velvet trim, silk robes, and a French-muslin chemise.

"Well, Gilbert Daniels wasn't peddling moonshine," Fargo said. "Looks like Cody Jeffries has got himself a fancy-piece, all right—a damned expensive one. First time I ever heard of a small-town sheriff who can keep a mistress in silk and satin."

"The hell you think she's up to?" Cranky Man wondered. "Seems like Felicity Meadows would get her a rich daddy in some big city back east."

"Trying to figure out a woman's mind," Fargo replied, "is like trying to figure out what existed before once upon a time. She might have nothing to do with the crimes and just likes the money. Hell, Jeffries could be innocent, too. I'm assuming that until I know different."

"He could be," Cranky Man echoed, not sounding too convinced.

They quickly searched the rest of the house, Fargo grinning when Cranky Man filched an old envelope and stuck it in his pocket.

"Maybe that's something important," Fargo remarked.

"Good. Better magic."

"Not a damn thing," Fargo declared when they'd finished. "I guess it was a wild hare of an idea. Still . . . what's Felicity's mix in all this?"

"Best way to find out," Cranky Man suggested, "is to get her to drop her linen for you."

Fargo mulled that. "I've had a little experience in that line. Might be a useful idea at that."

"Even if it ain't," Cranky Man said as they headed for the open window, "think of the fun you'll have, you lucky son of a bitch."

The sun was at his back and losing its heat when Fargo returned to the livery stable and stripped the tack from the Ovaro, turning him over to Dolomite for a rubdown and currycombing.

"I plan to roust you out early," he reminded Cranky Man. "And it might be a long day in the saddle, so don't get too cozy with the porcupine juice. Sleep on your weapons, too. The gang knows by now that you're siding me, and they might have heard my stretcher that you're an army scout. They could jump you at any time."

"Hell, I'm chicken-fixins. They'll kill you first, hair face."

"First, second, it won't matter—they want the pair. Stay sober tonight."

Fargo opted for the middle of wide Main Street as he hoofed it back to the Razorback. It made him more visible, but eliminated the close-in ambush. Just before he reached the front doors of the saloon, he ducked into the alley and went around to the back stairs.

There was a bare patch of sandy soil at the foot of the stairs. It showed a confusion of footprints from men frequenting the whores upstairs. Fargo dropped down on one knee and studied the patterns, patiently sorting them out.

He spotted a familiar print: a left heel with a chunk missing, leaving a slightly raised ridge. The same print made by whoever tried to blow up his room. It was recent, judging from the strong edges, and led toward the stairs but not away.

Meaning whoever it was had either left by the front entrance of the saloon or was still up there, Fargo realized. But was he here to ride the soiled doves or to kill the Trailsman?

Fargo cast one last glance around in the fading light and moved quickly but silently up the stairs. He peeked through the open door on the landing and down the candlelit hallway. It was still early enough that no line had formed. He skinned back his Colt and started toward his room at the far end of the hall.

Lynette's door creaked open. "Skye! I thought you just went in your room? I heard the key—"

118

She fell silent when she spotted his gun. Fargo touched a finger to his lips, nudging her back into her room. He moved down toward his door. Staying to one side, he keyed the lock.

Even though he'd expected it, the sudden, loud gunshot made him flinch. The bullet punched through the door and into the wall behind him, causing a puff of plaster dust. Five more shots followed in rapid succession, stitching a pattern of holes across the door.

Fargo slumped loudly to the floor, propped up on his left elbow with his gun pointed at the pockmarked door. The rattling click of a cylinder told him the would-be assassin was reloading. Fargo thumbed his hammer back, waiting.

The door exploded outward and Fargo glimpsed gleaming consumptive eyes in a furtive face. The Colt bucked in his fist, and a thin rope of blood coiled from Scout Langley's forehead. He took two shambling steps, then was a corpse before he hit the floor in an awkward heap.

Fargo had to scramble to avoid the rapidly pooling blood. Lynette poked her head out. "You all right, Skye?"

"Still sassy and handsome," he assured her. "But from now on Scout Langley will be having his mail delivered by moles."

"Good! He likes to cut his whores."

The soiled doves and a couple of johns ventured out into the hallway. Fargo stepped over the body and into his room, making sure it was clear. The acrid stench of burnt powder assaulted his nostrils, and the smoke was so thick it billowed through the open door.

Mackenzie wasn't going to like this, he realized, but Fargo didn't see that he had many options. On the credit side of the ledger, this made three of the original gang members who were now out of the holdup business.

Fargo glanced at a tall redhead who was dressed to go out. "Hon, do me a favor? Will you run across the street to the undertaker's parlor and tell Artemius Ward he's needed up here? And tell him I want you to have the two-dollar bonus he promised me."

The soiled dove hurried off just as Cody Jeffries appeared. He looked at the body, half in and half out of the room, then at Fargo.

"Waited for you in your room, right? I can see from the outward splintering of the door that the shots were fired from inside."

Fargo nodded, and Jeffries cast a heavy sigh. "Well, this is your first killing in Pine Hollow. And I don't see that you had much choice. Fargo, no offense, but I'll be a happy man when you and that featherhead friend of yours light a shuck out of here."

But why? Fargo wondered. *To restore the peace, or so you can run your criminal empire unmolested?*

"And I'll be a happy man," Fargo replied, "if I *can* light a shuck outta here."

Sunday dawned overcast and gloomy, but Fargo stuck to his plan. The Sloan brothers had to be hiding their horses somewhere in the area. And even with three of their men now dead or in jail, and one outlaw horse dead, there should be four horses left. Fargo had described the horses he saw in a written report filed last Tuesday with Colonel Mackenzie.

"Here's what I don't savvy," Cranky Man said as they tacked their mounts at the livery. "So what if we do locate their horses? They ain't gonna carry a brand—how do we prove who the riders are?"

Fargo centered his saddle and tightened the cinch. "Use your think-piece. There's wolves and bears in this part of the state, and an outlaw's horse will have to be grained every day so it can run fast and long. And unless there's a corral, which I doubt, they'll have to be tethered and exercised—they want those mounts in top shape."

"I take your drift. Somebody's tending to them."

"Now you're whistling. And it won't be one of the outlaws—those lazy sons of bitches live in saloons, not under the stars."

Cranky Man untangled his bridle reins. "So whoever it is, you get him to sing?"

Fargo nodded. "If he can read, I . . . persuade him to sign a statement. We might also get some idea when the gang plans to pick their horses up next. Sheriff Jeffries and some provost soldiers would have enough proof to arrest them when they show up. I admit it's a long shot."

"Plenty of open country around here," Cranky Man pointed out. "We can't search all of it."

"The Indian Territory is just west of us, and only a damn fool would leave good horseflesh there. They miss nothing more than their herds."

"Damn straight," Cranky Man said. "With these ration cuts lately by the Indian Bureau, they got no meat."

"Fort Bowman is to the north," Fargo added, "with water scarce and soldiers patrolling. I'd say we need to look south or east of here."

"Ain't you got army maps?"

"Most of 'em are useless. The only maps the War Department supplies are outline maps. They show nothing about the actual terrain. So I make my own maps in my head."

Fargo slid his Henry from its boot and checked the action. He slid it back into its sheath and swung up and over. He took a long look in every direction.

"By now the Sloan brothers must know I killed their cousin," he told Cranky Man. "These crackers are big on blood vengeance, so keep your eyes skinned. They got two reasons to kill me now."

Fargo remembered, from earlier times as a contract scout for the army, that the country just south of here included plenty of small rivers, creeks, lakes and ponds. They found an old wagon lane and headed due south.

"Me and Dolomite were frying fish last night," Cranky Man remarked, "when we heard the six gunshots. Soon as they stopped, Dolomite says, 'Aww, hell, Fargo's dead.' Then a single shot rings out, and I said, 'Aww, hell, Fargo's alive.'"

"You better be glad I'm still above the horizon, old son. You've already earned fifteen dollars so far. You can't collect unless I'm alive."

"If you get killed, can I have your Henry?"

Fargo nodded. "Take my horse, too, long as you promise not to eat him. For some strange damn reason, he likes you."

"Yeah, you get the women, I get the horses. How 'bout this Lynette? Did Jessie mean it when she said Lynette would sell it to a red man?"

"Tell you what—I'll put in a good word for you."

"In that case, I *am* glad you didn't get killed."

Fargo hooked right, leading them around a string of dry washes. The terrain hereabouts varied from meadows teeming with wildflowers to low, timber-covered hills. As they advanced south, both men kept a constant eye out for horses or troublesome ambush points.

They passed a few rustic dwellings, pine cabins or clapboard shanties with rickety privies out back. From one of the shanties emerged a bearded man in dingy long handles, a fowling piece in the crook of one arm.

"Mister," he said to Fargo, "what's that Injin doin' sportin' a rifle?"

"We're U.S. Army scouts," Fargo lied, "under orders from Colonel Mackenzie at Fort Bowman. Word has it a few bucks have jumped. They're not dangerous, but we plan to haze them back onto the rez."

"Glad to hear it. When them red sons ain't beggin', they're stealing my chickens."

"Goddamn savages," Cranky Man said. "I hear they hump their own mothers."

"Ain't got no hair around their peckers, neither," the rustic sage said, spitting an amber stream of tobacco juice onto the ground. "'Course, you'd know that."

Fargo waited until they were past the cabin before he gave vent to his laughter, Cranky Man joining him. The sky had cleared soon after sunrise, but Fargo felt the old arrow point in his back aching, and knew a storm was brewing.

The few horses he had spotted were swayback nags or big dobbins. Close to noon they stopped at a small pond with water bugs skimming over its surface. While their horses tanked up, Fargo circled the pond looking for sign that horses had been kept there.

"Nothing," he told Cranky Man. "A better place to keep horses would be in the bottomland near a river. Plenty of lush graze. The Danville River is straight ahead."

They gnawed on some hardtack and dried fruit before riding on. With ambush on his mind, Fargo avoided trails that dipped into valleys, instead riding the divides between them. Eventually they emerged from the hills onto a fertile plain that descended toward the Danville. Sandbar willows all along the river could easily have hidden attackers, but Fargo chanced them anyway, intent on locating those horses.

They worked their way around a bend in the river and spotted a surveyor hunched over a theodolite. Fargo raised one hand high in the frontier sign of friendly intent and they rode in closer.

"Howdy," Fargo called from the saddle. "By any chance you spotted a small group of horses tethered or corralled in this area?"

The surveyor, a young man whose face was peeling from sunburn, shook his head. "I sure haven't, friend. Saw a few mules, is all."

"Thanks," Fargo said, starting to gig the Ovaro forward.

"Hey!" the surveyor called. "I'm sighting a bed for a proposed short-line railroad between Little Rock and Fort Bowman. My assistant's laid up from a rattlesnake bite, and I need a man to hold the sticks for me. Pays a dollar a day and meals. Either one of you interested?"

"Wish we could help you," Fargo said. "We're on a job for the army right now. First I've heard that a railroad's pushing out to Fort Bowman."

The surveyor looked glum. "Well, it's trying, anyhow. But it's one damn delay after another, and old man Mackenzie is having a conniption fit. He just might go bust before we even grade all the bed."

Fargo exchanged a puzzled glance with Cranky Man. "Mackenzie? You don't mean Colonel Linton Mackenzie?"

"No, his brother, Randolph. He's a land speculator and budding railroad tycoon. Colonel Mackenzie managed to steer the contract to him, but you ask me, the bid was too low. Randolph has been forced to sell some assets to keep the project alive."

"Good luck," Fargo said, riding on.

Cranky Man nudged his skewbald abreast of the Ovaro. "The hell's an asset?" he asked.

Fargo ignored the question, lost in rumination. "Me and the colonel ain't exactly swapping spit," he finally said. "So it ain't peculiar that I never heard of his brother. But seems like he woulda mentioned this railroad headed toward the fort."

"Maybe not," Cranky Man suggested, "if his brother might be going broke over it. Might be ashamed of him or worried it could hurt his own job in the army."

"That rings right," Fargo agreed. "That's the colonel—stiff-necked pride."

After another hour of fruitless searching, the sweaty and dusty men reined in at a natural pool in the river. They sprawled on the low, grassy bank and plunged their heads under the water, the cold shock reviving them. Fargo took in a mouthful, rinsed his mouth, then spat it out and drank deeply.

They dropped their horses' bridles and led them in to drink. Fargo grinned when he saw Cranky Man return to the bank and practice one of the few Indian customs he still honored—"pissing respectfully" to avoid all living things.

"What happens if you piss on a bug?" he teased the Choctaw. "You go to Indian hell?"

"The only hell we got was a gift from the white man—the reservations."

"Well, you won that hand," Fargo surrendered. "Let's ford the river and reverse our dust."

Before he swung up into leather Fargo checked his saddle and pad for burrs and inspected his cinches, latigos, stirrups, bridle and reins. He had just grabbed the horn, ready to swing up onto the hurricane deck, when the hawthorn bushes on his left suddenly rustled.

"Cover down!" he told Cranky Man in a hoarse whisper.

Both men dove for a dead log nearby. Fargo shucked out his Colt and knocked the thong off the hammer, cocking it.

The bushes rustled again, and this time Fargo could see them moving. He brought his gun hand out over the log and drew a bead on the spot.

Moments later, a skunk waddled out and headed for the river.

"Fargo, your nerves are strung too tight," Cranky Man roweled him. "It's just an essence peddler."

"I am a little hair-trigger right now," Fargo admitted. "That's what comes of five attempts on my life in six days."

They forded and headed west along the opposite bank, scouring the landscape as far as they could see. The slow, thorough search turned up no outlaw horses.

By late afternoon Fargo pointed toward the sky. "See them sheep clouds making up? Gonna be a helluva gully washer. We best head back."

They followed a different route so they could search more ground. The cloud-choked sun set without fanfare, and heat lightning flashed out ahead of them. Fargo switched hands on the reins to ease his cramped muscles. He figured they were still ten miles from town.

"Sun going low and no supper," Cranky Man groused.

"Next time I'll bring a sugar tit for you. Break out your slicker—it's about to pour."

They were barely slickered against the rain when, abruptly, the dark and sagging sky opened up. Huge, heavy drops of rain mixed with hail battered man and horse, and Fargo's only guide in the gathering darkness were occasional flashes of lightning.

Soon the horses were splashing through mud as thick and sloppy as gumbo. Rumbling thunder rocked the ground as the dim lights of Pine Hollow finally glimmered into view.

"Just wasted our damn time!" Cranky Man shouted above the racket of rain and wind.

But Fargo, who had done plenty of thinking during the ride back, wasn't so sure about that. Sometimes a man went digging for silver and turned up gold. . . .

12

Monday dawned warm and clear, and by noon Main Street had dried out from the night's storm. Fargo and Cranky Man had eggs and scrapple at the Half Moon and took a sack of warm corn dodgers back to the livery for Dolomite.

"Mighty kind of you, Mr. Fargo," Dolomite said, flashing his gap-toothed grin. "I generally makes my own, but Tubby put bacon in his."

"Dolomite," Fargo said, "if you wanted to hide five horses in this area, where would you do it?"

The liveryman pondered that as he chewed his food. "If they was a man tending to them, I might choose woods. Plenty of trees here 'bouts, and ain't nobody could see 'em from the roads. Now, a horse don't like trees—it's open spaces they favor so's they can see danger in time to run. But I ain't never knowed of any outlaws to care what horses likes."

"Trees," Fargo said, mulling it. "Why not? I never even considered woods, but that would allow the gang to keep them close by."

Cranky Man tipped his hip flask, looking disgusted. "You don't need to tell me—tack my horse. We're riding out to beat the trees."

Fargo nodded. "We'll spread out in a circle from the Sloan boys' shack. But first I'm stopping by the jailhouse. Be ready to hit leather when I come back."

"Speakin' of them Sloan boys," Dolomite spoke up, "you be mighty careful, Mr. Fargo. Butch and Romer, them two be swaggerin' it around town, braggin' how they gone avenge they cousin Scout."

"That so? Where they at—the Stardust?"

Dolomite nodded.

"All right," Fargo said. "Think I'll pay them a mourning call. Seems the decent thing to do."

Fargo crossed the street and walked down to the Stardust Tavern, a seedier version of the Razorback and the saloon that catered to the criminal element as well as the general riffraff. He pushed open the batwings and immediately spotted Butch Sloan's low-crowned shako hat. He and Romer stood at the raw plank bar, sharing a bottle.

"I hear you two sissy-bitches been pissing out your eyes over your skinny runt of a cousin," Fargo announced as he walked toward them.

Both men glanced over their shoulders, faces blank with surprise.

"Way I see it," Fargo added, "your murdering cousin is right where he belongs—six feet closer to hell. And I'm proud to have put him there."

Butch's granite-hard, beard-smudged face tightened with seething rage. "You shouldn't ought to've done that, Fargo. Won't be long, and you'll buy the farm, bull and all."

"That's gaudy patter." Fargo stopped right in front of the pair. "Why wait? Here's your chance to buck me out in smoke—powder-burn me at point-blank range. Two against one—jerk 'em back."

Neither man, seeing the steely determination in Fargo's eyes, seemed inclined to accept his invitation.

"Can't blame you for being pissed at me," Fargo goaded. "With Baxter and Jonas jugged, and Scout feeding worms, that's three killers you have to find for your holdup gang."

"You got it bass-ackwards, Fargo," Romer said. "Everybody knows *you're* the lead stallion in this holdup gang."

"That's saloon gossip you started, but it got shot down on Saturday when you pulled that job near Booneville and I was in court. The worm has started to turn, boys."

Butch's thin lips eased back from his crooked, yellow teeth. "You know, Romer? If a man shoots a stallion just right, it will never sire again."

In a heartbeat, the muzzle of Fargo's Colt was tucked tight into Sloan's family jewels. The menacing click of the hammer made sweat bead on the loudmouth's face.

"Jesus G-G-God, Fargo, *don't* pull that trigger! I was only funnin'!"

"More gaudy patter, huh? Get this straight in that ugly gourd of yours, Butchie boy. Whatever happens to my stallion will happen to you, and that's a straight-arrow promise from the Trailsman. Savvy that?"

"I savvy."

Fargo kept his shooter aimed as he backed out of the saloon, then leathered it and watched his back-trail as he walked down to the jailhouse. Sheriff Jeffries, looking unkempt and disconsolate, sat at a battered kneehole desk reading reward dodgers. Jonas Wheeling and Baxter Sanford were visible in the small cell behind him, playing cards on the floor.

"Fargo," the lawman greeted him, "I'm glad you beat the charges on Saturday, but did you have to put these two hyenas in jail for perjury? I sleep on a straw shakedown and wash up at the livery. Hell, I can't even change clothes."

Or top your beautiful woman, Fargo thought.

"Fargo, you crusading son of a bitch," Baxter called out. "We got friends. We'll both live to piss on your grave."

"Make sure you squat to do it," Fargo advised. "I know you females have a hard time aiming."

Fargo lowered his voice. "Sheriff, got any idea where the Sloan brothers and Scout were during this last heist?"

"I was curious about that, too. Gus, the barkeep at the Stardust, says they were there, gambling and drinking, until past noon."

"That saloon looks like a robbers' roost to me. This Gus—could he be bought?"

"Most men can be," Jeffries said. "A few of the regular customers also vouched for them."

"Let me guess—the Sloan boys are mighty generous at pouring the liquor?"

Jeffries nodded. "An alibi's an alibi even if I don't believe it. Speaking of men and their whereabouts—there was a fellow, Ike Siddons, who stopped by here yesterday morning to tell me he saw the three Ravenel brothers riding back from the direction of Booneville Saturday afternoon."

"You trust this man?"

"More or less. But he does drink at the Stardust."

Here it was again, Fargo thought—the sheriff was singling out the Ravenels, a clan Fargo was associated with through Jessie.

"Are you telling me," Fargo asked him, "that you don't believe those two shit-birds behind you are part of the gang? Even after I described Jonas's horse from the Tuesday holdup?"

"No, I believe they're guilty, all right. But they also know the Ravenel boys. In fact, I once arrested the five of them for selling whiskey to a grog shop on the reservation."

"I'll be damned," Fargo said, wondering if he'd been tricked by the entire Ravenel clan, Jessie included.

"What are you two lovebirds whispering about?" Baxter demanded.

"Stow it, mouthpiece," Jeffries shot back.

"I guess you know by now that I'm working for the army?" Fargo asked the sheriff.

Jeffries nodded.

"Did Colonel Mackenzie tell you?"

"Hell no. I just figured it out. Plenty of others have, too, since the trial Saturday. The questions you've been asking, and your history with the army, made it a safe bet."

For a moment Fargo was tempted to ask about the female clothing at the sheriff's house. But he wasn't eager to admit he'd entered the place without permission—or to show all his cards just yet. Even amiable men like Jeffries could turn killer in a heartbeat if a woman was involved.

He walked back to the cell. "You know, if you boys sign a detailed confession, naming *all* the men involved in this gang of yours, it might go easier on you down the road. There's gonna come a point where you'll be in an army stockade, and just think how they're going to treat you."

"Up yours, Fargo," Jonas spat at him. "Ain't nobody got *shit* on us for no holdups or killings. It's my word against yours about my horse being at the robbery."

"You'll crater," Fargo said calmly. "It's cowardice that drives most men to crime."

He bade the sheriff good day and started across the street toward the livery. A sudden drumbeat of hooves made him glance right toward the far end of town. A tall, lean soldier on a cavalry sorrel was leaving town. Fargo couldn't be sure it was James Hargrove, the dispatch rider, but he was the right size. And there appeared to be a mochilla, a leather mail pouch, flapping against his saddle fender.

Fargo's brow wrinkled in puzzlement. If that was Hargrove, sent to see him, he would have waited. And if he wasn't sent to see him, who, then? Certainly not Sheriff Jeffries.

"Curious," Fargo said aloud, heading for the livery.

Fargo and a reluctant Cranky Man spent most of Monday afternoon searching the heavy pine forests west of town. Twice the skewbald wiped Cranky Man from the saddle under a low-hanging branch, and Fargo had to threaten force to subdue the Choctaw's shouted oaths and swear words.

"We're just washing bricks," Fargo finally announced. "Let's give it up as a bad job."

"I knew it was a bad job when we started looking yesterday," Cranky Man said. "Ain't like you to look for a needle in a haystack."

Fargo grinned. "I admit I never expected to find their horses. I wanted to get the surrounding country fixed in my mind, and I wanted time to think about this thing."

"Have you cracked the nut?"

"Maybe, but I haven't exposed the meat. I'm not certain-sure just yet, and there's some sign I still can't read. But mainly, I think I've got this trail worked out."

"Then who's the lead stallion?"

While the two men spoke, Fargo never once interrupted his intent study of the shadowed pockets of forest surrounding them, giving the Ovaro his head in the dense trees.

"I won't say a name yet because I need more proof. But that's coming, old son."

Two hours later Fargo took in Felicity Meadows's three-song set at the Razorback. This time, however, her eyes sought, then challenged, Fargo's—a fact not wasted on a jealous Gilbert Daniels.

"See, Mr. Fargo?" the sharper complained, taking a seat at Fargo's table. "She's all eyes for you. God, she was so *obvious*. I thought a lady is supposed to be demure?"

"I see you learned nothing from our little talk," Fargo said, watching the way Fel's gown of emerald green taffeta lace bared her slim white shoulders. White satin slippers and gloves made her even more like a storybook vision.

Daniels leaned forward. "Yes, I did. I'm not cheating at poker now. But I'm still in love with her."

"What, one woman? If that's your choice, all right. I say love 'em all."

"A man can *do* that? Don't you ever, you know, care for some over others?"

"Oh, some ride higher in my memory than others. But not like you're doing with Fel. Look, a beautiful woman spells trouble, and sometimes trouble like that can be exciting. Other times, it's just trouble. And I got a hunch Fel's the worst kind of trouble."

"Looks like you're about to find out, Mr. Fargo—you lucky dog. She's headed toward your table."

"Does this mean you're going to challenge me to a duel, Romeo?"

"Nah, you'd just kill me, and besides, she's already consorting with the sheriff. You know, she *never* sits with customers. Damn it, I *am* going to practice your system. Love women, not woman."

Daniels returned to the poker table, and Fargo rose half out of his chair when Felicity stopped at his table, her hair now unpinned and flowing in wheat-colored waves over her back and shoulders. She looked so stunning that Fargo suddenly wished he could paint.

"Won't you have a seat, Miss Meadows?"

"I'm not sure," she replied, those striking green eyes studying him. "You know, Mr. Fargo, such a tall, broad-shouldered, slim-hipped man as you would look magnificent in some well-tailored clothing."

She fingered some fringes on his shirt. "These buckskins look so primitive. My stars!" She snatched her hand back. "Is that old blood in the fringes?"

Fargo nodded. "But most of it's animal blood."

"Well, you definitely need to catch up with the fashions. *Vestis virum reddit.*"

"I don't palaver the lingo."

"It's Latin. 'Clothes make the man.' "

Fargo laughed. "Maybe you know about clothing, but if you

really believe that, you don't know sic 'em about men. The worst swindlers, liars, cowards, thieves and murderers in the West are decked out in toppers and silk cravats."

Her pretty face turned thoughtful. "I believe you have a point there, Mr. Fargo."

She took the chair opposite his. "Do you enjoy my singing?"

"I've heard the best songbirds in San Francisco, New Orleans, and Saint Louis, and you're the top of the heap. I'd wager angels could take lessons from you."

"Well, in *singing*, perhaps," she said with a coy smile. "Most of my talents would be no good for an angel. But here I've just discovered that you have more culture than most of the philistines in this one-horse town."

"Say, I'm no professor."

"I'm not so sure. Within your sphere, Mr. Fargo, I'd call you an Oxford don."

"Oxford I've heard of, but not this fellow Don."

"That twinkle in those charming blue eyes tells me you're teasing me."

"No," he assured her. "That twinkle means something else."

After a confused moment she took his meaning. "Tush! Just because I've complimented you a little hardly means I want to . . . dally with you. Not that I find that prospect repugnant."

Fargo smiled, pretending her remark was just harmless flirting when in fact it was his bugle call to action.

"It does seem a mite queer," he remarked, "that a woman of your talent, tastes and bearing would stick around Pine Hollow. It's a long way from its first opera house."

The very tip of her tongue, moist and pink, peeked out through her lips before she answered. "There's something to be said, Mr. Fargo, for being a big fish in a little pond."

The woman was lying, and Fargo enjoyed the game she was playing with those lies. He also enjoyed her smooth-as-moonstone skin and those lips as luscious as ripe berries. But he also noticed everyone in the saloon watching them—including a jealous Jessie Ravenel and Gilbert Daniels.

"Another thing," Fargo said, "you told me only a man's bank account can get you interested. Why the exception in my case?"

"Women say a great many things they don't really mean. But

you're jumping to conclusions . . . Skye. I'm not part of that 'pig ranch' upstairs."

"No, but think about what they're doing up there, and then think about us doing it even better. My 'sphere,' as you call it, includes more than just drifting beyond the next ridge and getting my buckskins bloody."

"Yes, I've heard all about that, too. As for thinking about it . . . I have been since I first saw you at the livery, bloody buckskins and all."

"Well, then," Fargo said, "here's hoping thought kindles action."

She rose, and Fargo stood up with her, publicly catering to the great lady. The lively piano and fiddle music forced her to lean closer, and Fargo smelled her jasmine perfume.

"Perhaps there will be a message for you later," she murmured.

After Felicity had left by the rear door, Fargo spotted Jake Ravenel and his brothers sitting near the batwings. He bought three mugs of beer and thumped them down on their table.

"Would you gents take offense if I asked what you were doing on Saturday?"

Jake sniggered. "Nothing like what you'll be doing later tonight, you lucky son of a bitch. Fargo, you must put a hoodoo on the women."

"Who's accusing us this time?" Taylor asked.

"It's hints, not accusations," Fargo said. "I don't swallow them."

"We was brewing and delivering moonshine on Saturday," Lindsay Ravenel said.

"Good enough," Fargo said before he headed upstairs. But he couldn't help wondering if he'd been too hasty in taking these three off his list.

By now Fargo was convinced that Fel would indeed send for him. Her assignment was to gather information, to use her limitless powers of seduction to break down his caution and get him to spill his guts about the holdups—whatever he could prove or had guessed. And perhaps to lure him into yet another death trap.

He lay awake on his bed, one candle guttering in a wall sconce and his Colt flat across his chest. Out in the hallway, the tall case clock chimed the quarter hour. When three swift knocks sounded on his door, Fargo sat up.

"Who's there?"

"Hotel messenger, sir."

"All right, push it under the door."

A wax-sealed envelope slid into his room. Fargo put a quarter on the floor and kicked it under the door.

Her message was to the point:

Top floor, west side. Don't use front hotel entrance. Use rear employees' door, and make sure no one sees you. My door will be unlocked.

"Make sure no one sees you," Fargo repeated. The words a cautious lady could be expected to use when her reputation was on the line. But also if she wanted no witnesses that he was ever there should his dead body turn up somewhere.

Fargo used the rear staircase when he went outside. The Razorback was closed and the town as dead as the saloon. Fargo stood in the shadow of the Razorback and studied Pine Hollow's moon-bleached landscape. Then, staying behind the buildings, he walked down to the hotel.

He circled around back and inside the building, making it upstairs without being spotted. Fargo saw a door with a glass knob and let himself in.

The splendor of this huge drawing room stopped Fargo in his tracks. He took in an oval, rose-patterned rug, blue chintz easy chairs and loveseats, a black marble fireplace and embroidered fire screens, and several low tables holding fresh roses in cut-glass vases.

He could hear a woman humming at the end of a hallway on his left. Filling his hand, Fargo made a quick pass through the rest of the rooms. Then he returned and opened the hallway door again, shutting it loudly and locking it.

"Step down the hallway, Skye," Fel's melodic voice invited him. "I'm in the bedroom changing into something more comfortable."

Every sense keen, Fargo followed the long hallway. Wall candles reflected in the polish on the floor, making it glow bloodred like ruby embers. He found Felicity disrobing behind a three-panel screen.

"Well, you succeeded," she told him, favoring him with a dazzling smile. "It's all I've been able to think about."

She stepped out wearing only the thinnest of cotton wrappers. Even in the candlelight, Fargo could see the dark protuberances of her impressive nipples. As he stepped closer, however, she closed the wrapper at her throat and assumed a "proper" tone:

"But don't get the wrong idea about me. I am not the type to be kissed in dark corners like some wanton or to dispense my favors easily."

Fargo laughed. "Oh, you're silky satin, all right."

He crushed her in his arms and kissed her forcefully, feeling her go limp. She pulled back, and quite visibly her pulse leaped into her soft, white throat. Fargo watched a vein throb with her suddenly kindled desire.

He shucked off the wrapper, exposing a naked goddess from an erotic French painting. In the soft light her skin glowed like an angel's halo. Fargo's eyes feasted: breasts firm and high, with huge strawberry nipples; a hard but gently curving stomach and flaring hips.

Fargo pulled her toward a bed with a coverlet of intricate crochet work.

"No," she begged him. "I don't like a bed. Sit in the chair with me on top. That's how I imagined us doing it."

She pointed to a large chintz chair in the corner. Fargo, always flexible in the acrobatics of love, grinned his approval. They crossed to the chair and he dropped his gun belt, then his trousers. Her lips parted in approving surprise when she saw his curved saber leaping with his heartbeat.

"My goodness, Mr. Fargo, no wonder you ride a stallion. Now, may *I* ride one?"

She placed both hands on his chest and pushed him back into the chair. So excited that her breathing was raspy, she straddled his lap and gripped his manhood in a tight fist, bending him to the perfect angle before guiding him past the chamois folds at her portal and deeper to the tight walls of her love tunnel.

"*Oh* you fill a woman up," she cried, bouncing up and down and grinding her succulent globes into his face. "*So* full! It feels like you're up to my belly button!"

By flexing and unflexing his hip muscles, Fargo was able to buck her right up to the tip of his shaft and send her plunging back down, giving maximum pleasure to her swollen pearl and his swollen member.

Soon the chair was rocking, and Fel keening with pleasure, as hot, explosive passion took control of both of them. Each time she gasped with a climax, an even bigger one came exploding right behind it. When Fargo finally spent himself, the force of his concluding thrusts almost shot her from his lap.

They were motionless with paralytic stupefaction for long minutes, Fargo's mind a drifting blank as his body returned to normal.

"Well," she said, untangling from him and putting her wrapper back on, "how about a drink to cap that off?"

A table beside the chair held a carafe of whiskey and two glasses.

"So," she remarked casually as she poured the liquor, "the word about town is that you're looking into all these terrible holdups?"

"You know I am," Fargo said mildly. "Why bother to ask?"

"You needn't be brutal about it," she pouted, although Fargo could see she was also nettled.

"That's some nice clothing you've got out at Cody Jeffries's house," Fargo remarked, watching her from unblinking eyes.

"I? What—what clothing?" she faltered out, taken by surprise.

Fargo, busy buckling on his gun belt, laughed. "I figured as much. You were planning to gather information, not cough it up. What clothing? The expensive clothing you've got hanging in his bedroom—clothing only you could afford, with help from a man."

"I . . . how can you be absolutely certain it's mine?"

"Well," Fargo bluffed, "I've seen you ride out to his house more than once."

"Surely to God you can't be serious? *Me* and Cody Jeffries?"

"Among others."

"All right, your transparent stratagems are unnecessary. I'll simply be candid. I like manly men. And Sheriff Jeffries is a rich, manly man—a double attraction to a woman like me."

"There's likely some truth in that answer," Fargo said. "But he's the only one stupid enough to think it's a love affair."

She swept aside the comment, her pretty face suddenly pale. "Never mind Cody, that's over. You know, if you'll stop asking so many silly and personal questions, we could make what just happened here a regular arrangement."

"You're saying I should nail my colors to your mast? Fall under your spell like love-struck Cody has and neglect my job? Maybe even cross over to the lawless side? Lady, to tell you the straight, I got all I wanted from you when you spread those pretty legs for me one time."

"You'll want it again," she assured him. "You'll burn for me. No man has *ever* tasted love with me and walked away."

Fargo glanced around at the opulence and then recalled the stark images of the murdered men last Tuesday, flies buzzing in their blood. Bile erupted up his throat.

"You and your partner figured no one would much give a shit about the death of single men who live in barracks, didn't you? Just like you can put silk next to your overrated quim and play the great lady. Truth is, you're lower than any whore living over the Razorback."

She began pacing next to the bed. "Fargo, what is wrong with you and what doctor told you so? This is just insane prattle!"

"Bottle it, sugar tits. What message did the dispatch rider bring you today?"

Her face stiffened and she stopped pacing. "I don't happen to like these questions."

"What message did he bring you?"

She reached under one of the pillows and produced a Colt Pocket Model. "All I have to do is shoot you and say you forced your way in here. Every man in town is in love with me."

"True. But before you paper the walls with my brains, you best ease off and consider this: I left your note, and the envelope with your seal, with Dave. You invited me here, late at night, and that'll be a helluva scandal when the ink-slingers get ahold of it. They like to write about me. And, darlin', there'll be legions of bereaved women looking to gut you."

Fargo's lies like truth gave her pause. He walked over and plucked the weapon from her hand. "You're not the murdering type, anyway, or you'd have carried out your orders by now. After, of course, riding me in the chair."

"I have no orders, you smug bastard."

"Yes, you do. I want that message," he told her, his tone cold and hard. "And if you don't give it to me, I'll break that lovely neck of yours. That's a cast-iron promise."

She gazed into his implacable blue eyes and shuddered at the power they radiated—a power born of unshakable will and sense of purpose.

"Give it," he said.

As if in a stupor, she crossed to a little cherrywood desk and opened the top drawer. She removed a folded sheet of foolscap and, hand trembling, gave it to him.

"I don't know why I didn't throw it away by now," she muttered, clearly bitter at herself.

"Before I open this," he told her, "let me give you some advice. You better come to Jesus right now because it's almost over and the hemp party is about to commence. Stop cooperating with the criminals and get ready to cooperate with a military tribunal. A woman like you won't stand before the gavel—not in Arkansas—so long as you weren't part of the actual crimes. If you're called as a witness, tell what you know and you'll be spared—you know what to leave out. That's why I'm not going to ask you who you've been working with—then I won't have to repeat it under oath in a public trial."

"So just now—you wouldn't have broken my neck?" she whispered.

"Lady, you spend too much time around criminals. The bluff was enough. Besides, I think I owe you one because I'm guessing you didn't carry out tonight's order. Let's see if I'm right."

Fargo opened the folded sheet. The three-word message was written in longhand and unsigned:

Kill him tonight.

13

"How are you, Fargo?"

"Tolerable well, Colonel."

Linton Mackenzie, seated at his desk with his hands folded on the blotter, watched the unexpected arrival from suspicious, fearful eyes. "I thought you were supposed to communicate with the fort by dispatch rider?"

"Yeah, well, I missed him yesterday when he was in town."

"Missed him?"

"Yeah. Seems he went to the hotel, but not the saloon."

Dread stirred within Fargo as the moment arrived to tip his hand. *Pile on the agony,* he thought. He pulled the folded sheet of paper from his possibles bag and dropped it on the desk.

Mackenzie recognized it immediately and stiffened. But he chose to pretend it wasn't there. His next remark told Fargo how desperate the man was to deny this fateful moment was happening.

"Fargo, I've heard about these shooting frays you've been in. I asked you to just get a scent—be subtle with this assignment."

"Yeah, but you didn't tell me why."

"The why was obvious—security."

"Security for you and Butch Sloan, you mean."

"Fargo, you're listening to more rumors," Mackenzie protested. "I hardly know Butch Sloan's name."

"That little note in front of you—'Kill him tonight.' I compared it to the dispatch you sent me in the Nebraska Territory. A perfect handwriting match. You were the brains behind the operation, Colonel. Three of the original gang are dead or behind bars, and I've got my sights notched on the other two. And I hate to tell you this, but I'm going to make sure you dance on air."

Fargo, still standing, watched Mackenzie carefully, for this was a dangerous moment. For a long time *he* had held the whip hand. Now the lash was turned against him, and all his big schemes had turned into mere mental vapors. That could force a man's hand before he even thought about it.

"Kill who? The word 'him' isn't worth much in a court of law, Fargo."

"It's worth everything to me. Now it's all unraveling, and there'll be plenty more evidence to go with this. It's over, Colonel."

Slowly, deliberately, Mackenzie unsnapped his service holster and drew his Colt Army revolver. Fargo had no intention of shooting him—not on an army post where he'd likely be gunned down before he could explain.

"I hate to have to kill you, Fargo. But I know you. Only death will shut you up."

"Put it away from your mind, Colonel. I requested a couple of witnesses. Look out the window behind you."

Mackenzie slewed around in his chair. Sergeant Manning and Corporal Lofley, two of the troopers who had confronted Fargo a little over a week ago, stood watching.

Mackenzie's shoulders slumped under the weight of defeat. "You've caught me flat-footed, Fargo, and I don't know what to say. Twenty-seven years in the army tossed right down a rat hole. And I just made the list for promotion to general. Jesus Christ, what have I done?"

"Colonel, I can understand a soldier getting into money troubles—especially when your brother is sinking on a big railroad project that you talked the army into giving him. But killing your own men—how could a commanding officer do that?"

Mackenzie spoke as if the words were being wrenched out of him. "Clearly you know all of it, Fargo. They say a fish rots from the top, and I'm proof of that. The whole story I gave you was moonshine. I didn't want to hire you in the first place, knowing your caliber, but I had no choice. The War Department wanted you specifically, and I had to make it look good. I figured Fel—"

He paused and averted his eyes.

"You figured Fel could lure me in with her charms and kill me. That I grasp. But how could a C.O. kill his own men?"

"Fargo, it's not something a man can easily lay the tongue to.

My brother, Randolph, always has to be the biggest toad in the puddle, and I have never been able to say no to his various schemes. First I skirted regulations in landing his contract; then I sank my personal fortune in his short-line project. I was just throwing good money after bad."

Mackenzie looked at the revolver in his hand and placed it on his desk. "My motive was never to profit, Fargo, never. I wanted to save my brother and myself. There was the shame that failure would bring on me and my family, the destruction of my military career, perhaps even a court-martial and prison."

"And you were afraid of losing Felicity, right? The high-toned woman with expensive tastes and the go-between for you and the gang?"

Mackenzie visibly flinched at hearing her name. "There's no fool like an old fool," he admitted. "I met her at the officer's spring ball last year, and I embezzled funds from the quartermaster account to keep her in the manner I felt she deserved. Sheriff Jeffries was a thorn in my side because he was a conscientious peace officer."

"Until you had Fel distract him from his duties?"

Mackenzie nodded. "I knew he was head over heels. No man can resist her."

"The munitions and supplies you sold outright," Fargo added, "and you probably made deals with some merchants in Hog Town for unloading the U.S. script, right?"

"Yes, no questions asked by *that* bunch."

"Are there more holdups in the works?" Fargo asked.

"Nothing I'm a part of. So far they've acted only when I supply routes and dates. But Butch and Romer Sloan are loose cannons, and I've been fearing for some time that they'll strike on their own."

Mackenzie finally met his eyes. "So what's next? You plan to march me over to the provost marshal?"

Fargo shook his head. "You need to be a man and write down a full confession. There's still an honorable soldier inside you. The truth is coming out anyway, so take charge and do this last thing right. I'll sit and wait."

Mackenzie nodded. "Yes, it's high time I confessed. It's been gnawing at my guts for months. I don't even have the stomach for my own crimes."

He pulled out a sheet of regimental stationery, dipped a steel nib, and started to compose his shameful admission.

"Mention all the names you need to," Fargo said, "except for . . . a certain woman."

Mackenzie mustered a rueful smile. "So she got to you, too, eh?"

"No, they never do—I just play along with her kind and see where it takes me. But so far there's never been a woman hanged in the West, and that's a record I respect. I don't even believe in sending a woman to prison."

The disgraced officer spent the next fifteen minutes on his statement. He set the steel nib back in its inkpot, blotted the page, folded and sealed it. Then he handed it to Fargo.

"Why don't you deliver this for me?" Mackenzie said. "And will you leave me my gun?"

Fargo had expected this moment. He nodded. "Good-bye, Colonel. You gave some mighty good service, and I respect that. But you headed up a plot that killed your own troopers, and if that God you say you believe in is real, you're likely hell-bound."

Fargo was about twenty feet from the headquarters building when a single gunshot sounded from inside. He slowed in mid-stride, aware that another life had just been wasted by choosing the criminal path over the straight and narrow. Heavy of heart, discouraged by the human vanities, Fargo carried Mackenzie's confession to the provost marshal's office.

"You *knew* Mackenzie was going to kill himself?" Cranky Man's lopsided mouth showed his confusion. "You said you worked with this bluecoat before, that he was a good leader."

"That's past. He made his choice, and the shame still left in him couldn't let him face the army he betrayed. Stiff-necked pride . . . yeah, I figured he'd do it. It was a good choice. Saves the cost and further shame of a court-martial."

"Hell, I guess you're right. His medicine went bad, but he did one last decent thing. Say, you got any panther piss? I'm drier than a year-old cow chip."

"I'll pick you up some later. Hell, a baby don't holler for milk as much as you cry for whiskey."

The two men were keeping an eye on the town from the paddock in front of the livery barn. Fargo had quickly rubbed the

Ovaro down from shoulder to knee, but the pinto was restless for a good run and quivered, now and then, with barely controlled wildness.

"Anyhow," the Choctaw said, leaning against the middle corral pole and watching his horse roll, "you were a mutton-headed fool to go to the fort and slap his face with it. The Utes got a saying: 'Don't go looking for your own grave.'"

"Bully for them. Fargo's got a saying, too: 'Always surprise, confuse, and mystify your enemies.' I set events in motion today, that's all."

He took a good, long look down Main Street, which had not yet filled and thickened with locals and outlanders. A copper sunset blazed out on the rim of creation, and their faces seemed to flicker in the uncertain light.

"The thing I don't get," Cranky Man said, "is what first made you think of Mackenzie? You never said nothing."

"It was something the dispatch rider said about the colonel— that he didn't trust the telegraph. Most commanders do, so I got to wondering *why* the old soldier didn't want me using it. Maybe because I might mention something that could incriminate him later. It would do little good to kill me once I'd put damning evidence on record. The rest I got from that surveyor and then Fel."

"Yeah, makes sense." Cranky Man cleaned a fingernail with a matchstick. "Anyhow, Jonas and Baxter are starting to crack. They told Cody that one of the replacement riders, for the heist last Saturday, was Lester Trilby. Recall him?"

"Sure. He's the bullyboy, tried to drive us out of town on our first day here. The one bragging on the notches in his gun."

"Yeah. And it was Lester who kept the horses for them on his farm. Kept 'em in a barn by day, grazed them after dark. Cody gave Jonas and Baxter a bottle of rotgut for that information. The net is closing."

"Sure," Fargo agreed. "But the last to get caught in it will be Butch and Romer. The soldiers won't be hitting leather too quick—they have to work through military channels and with civilian law. And don't forget how those two have tried to kill us. We're in this thing, like it or not."

"Sounds like you're telling me *we* have to kill them."

"All right, so killing's not our first choice," Fargo said. "But it'll be a damn close second. Eventually, they'll get wind of Mackenzie's death and confession, and with the fat in the fire, they might make a long escape. I say let's just hunt 'em down before they head out, and powder-burn 'em. I don't like letting some son of a bitch just try to kill me from ambush."

"I'm in it," Cranky Man said. "But, Fargo, there's trouble brewing for us. This morning I woke up early, and I saw the sun coming up while a full moon was setting—that's consequential."

"Could be," Fargo agreed. "And it might be coming true right now. Here comes the sheriff. From the look on his face, this could get interesting."

"Be ready to draw," Cranky Man warned. "Lookit that red face—looks like he spent the last hour trying to move a stubborn turd. Shit, he knows about you and Felicity."

Cody Jeffries, a bull on the charge, bore down on the two men, spurs chinging, muscular arms swinging hard.

"Fargo!" he roared. "Fargo, you better—"

Hidden rifles—four of them, according to Fargo's wilderness-trained ear—shattered the early twilight when they sent lead hurling in at Fargo, Cranky Man, and Cody Jeffries. Trapped, all three men ate dirt and grass as the marksmen, firing from the mouth of an alley across the street, kept up a barrage of lead. Bullets chipped the corral poles and punched into the barn.

The bullet-savvy Ovaro stood stoic while horses inside the corral bucked and reared, their commotion driving Dolomite outside. Fargo managed to draw his Colt, but ground-skimming bullets made it a losing bet to return fire now. He had few targets from ground level, just the steady orange spears of muzzle flash.

"Dolomite!" he called back. "Can you stay out of sight and work the rifle in my scabbard?"

Dolomite, hunched down in the office doorway, nodded. "I seen it done."

He ran inside, a stray bullet chasing him.

"Christ, Fargo," Sheriff Jeffries jeered from his prone position, "I like Dolomite, but I doubt he could hit a tent from the inside."

"Won't matter," Fargo said. "We want a lot of firepower to drive them off, and sometimes noise is enough. Once that Henry gets their interest, the three of us will open up with our short guns."

Dolomite knelt at one side of the open doorway, his face in shadows, and opened fire. He held the weapon incorrectly, Fargo noticed, bracing the stock against his ribs instead of his shoulder socket. His shots were mostly inaccurate, but he was fast at levering and firing, just what Fargo wanted.

"Now!" he ordered, and all three men took advantage of the lull in enemy fire to rise up on one knee and add their fusillade to Dolomite's. Cranky Man's Dragoon kicked so hard that it almost toppled him backward. But the large-caliber slugs slapped into the wood warehouse near the alley entrance with a sound like small cannonballs.

By the time all four men expended their ammunition, black smoke hazed the area. But no more fire spat from the mouth of the alley.

"They decided to rabbit," Fargo said. "Looks like nobody wanted to hang around when Dead-eye Dolomite commenced firing. But this never happened, right?"

"Never did," the liveryman agreed enthusiastically. "I don't think they seen me, neither. A colored man shooting a gun at white men? Shoo!"

"Look," Fargo muttered to Cranky Man, "I can't have lead flying all over town on our account."

"On *your* account. I'm just a harmless drunk."

"Slice it any way you want to," Fargo said. "We're going to find a campsite outside of town. It's too easy for them to chuck lead here. And then we're gonna put paid to this Sloan account."

Cody Jeffries caught the tail end of Fargo's last sentence. "Speaking of putting paid to accounts, Fargo, I want to see you over at the jailhouse *right now.*"

The sheriff crossed the street in rapid strides and made sure the alley was clear before entering the jailhouse and leaving the door open for Fargo. Fargo followed at a more cautious pace, wary of a second attack on the heels of the first.

Fargo stepped inside the small, man-smell-reeking jailhouse and had to pull up short to avoid colliding with Jeffries.

"You know, Fargo," he greeted him from a face hard as a stone slab, "it's best to check the brand before you haze off another man's heifer."

Fargo had never seen such a big man move so swiftly. He

never saw the sledgehammer fist coming, either, but felt pain grate like a rasp as Jeffries drove a lightning-fast right uppercut. It lifted Fargo's toes off the floor and turned his legs rubbery. He did a Virginia reel but stayed on his feet.

The mild-mannered sheriff had suddenly turned as rough as a badger out of its hole. He waded into Fargo, blindly throwing one-two punches. The Trailsman, still rattled from the uppercut, sidestepped a few punches before rattling Jeffries with a round-house right.

"Who you rootin' for?" Jonas Wheeling asked his cohort.

"Don't make no never mind to me," Baxter Sanford replied. "I hate both them bastards."

"Yeah, but it was Fargo's courtroom bull that put us here."

"Yeah!" Baxter said. "*Whump* that cockchafer, Cody!"

"Knock this school-yard shit off, Cody," Fargo said even as Jeffries lunged for him. "Sheriff, we've both been bamboozled. Felicity Meadows was in league with Colonel Mackenzie."

The words hit Jeffries like buckshot. "Fel what?"

"Mackenzie masterminded the holdups. Fel had a number of jobs, one of which was to play you for a sap—to get information on what you knew and to keep you from doing your job. Macken-zie knew you were usually a good lawman, and he didn't want you doing too much investigating."

Jeffries stood with his fists up, the world-shaking words sink-ing in. The anger bled from his face, replaced by stunned wonder-ment. His fists dropped to his side, and he stood there breathing hoarsely from his exertions. The poor, foolish son of a bitch had fallen for it all the way, Fargo thought.

"You *believe* that about Fel?" he asked Fargo.

"To the marrow of my bones. But her name was left out of the confession Mackenzie wrote today. I hope you'll leave it out, too, in your report and testimony."

Jeffries sat down on the corner of his desk. "Fargo, you've given me a bad wrench. You're *sure* about this?"

Fargo nodded. "She herself gave me the evidence."

"What else did she give you?" the jealous man demanded.

"We never got around to that," Fargo lied. "Not after I con-fronted her."

"Well, don't that cap the climax? And me thinking . . . hell, it

146

should have been clear to aught but fancy that she was up to something. Jesus God, she played me all along."

Fargo swiped some blood off his lips. "There's no such thing as 'clear' when a beautiful girl is in the mix."

"I knew it didn't add up," Jeffries mused aloud, "no matter how I ciphered it. No woman half that good-looking ever noticed me before. But like a green-antlered fool, I fell hard."

"You ignored your job," Fargo reminded him. "Maybe you didn't break any serious laws, but falling for . . . a certain woman became your entire job, not looking out for the public safety. Thinking about her day and night, you didn't ask the obvious questions."

"I knew all that," Jeffries agreed, "but went on doing it anyway. That ambush on us just now—the Sloan boys got that up. I've known they're the road agents since Jonas and Baxter got arrested, but for too damn long I dismissed the Sloans and Scout as small potatoes. Christ, if I'd had anything on my mind besides—"

"Besides a certain lady," Fargo cut him off. "You got snookered other ways, too. Those 'alibis' the gang bragged on were all store-bought, and so were the lying witnesses who placed the Ravenels near the robberies. Hell, all these witnesses drink at the Stardust, and times are hard around here."

"Yeah," Jeffries said, his voice contrite. "The Ravenels . . . that was sheer stupidity and fever for a woman made me do that. When Mackenzie told me they were high on his list, I took the easy way out and suspected them myself. Hell, Felicity was all over me then, acting man hungry. I had no time for boring peace-keeping duties."

"Yeah," Fargo said impatiently, not interested in the self-pity, "but tell me this: on my first day in town, I got into a little dustup with the Sloans, and right after that I saw you in the alley with them, giving them the dickens. Why in the alley?"

"I rarely give a man the rough side of my tongue in public. Why berate a man in front of his friends and give him something to stew on? I was just telling them to settle down, for all the use my advice was."

"Your family—you *do* come from wealth?"

"My old man helps me out, and he can spare it—he owns a

cattle farm outside Little Rock. He added a cannery and packages beef for the army and wagon outfits. Fel knew that and made a big deal about how it's 'new money'—earned instead of inherited. Now I see why she admitted it—she *wanted* me to think she was after my money. That's something a man can understand, but the other . . . Christ. Cold-blooded murder."

"Aww, ain't that too suckin' bad," Jonas called out from behind bars. "Sheriff done lost his quality poon."

"Yeah, from now on he's holding his own," Baxter jeered. "Like us."

Fargo looked at both prisoners. "Are you soft-brains or just assholes? It's the knot for both of you, and sooner than you think."

His gaze cut to Jeffries again. "I was you, I'd put her away from my thoughts. It wasn't personal—women are just the way they are, especially the beauties. You ain't no sap in this. You enjoyed something every man in town wants, and, mister, you enjoyed it plenty. I wouldn't feel like a fool even though you know you were. Don't kill her, Cody. She doesn't deserve it, and you'll swing. Two lives wasted."

Fargo headed toward the door, studying the shadows beyond it. "Do what you have to with the Sloans," Fargo said just before he left. "I'm not giving up on them."

"Mackenzie's dead, so your work is finished."

Fargo shook his head. "I was never signed out from duty, so I'm still working for the army on these holdups. And I'm in a mood to hunt."

14

Fargo made good, that very night, on his decision to leave town. He relied on one of his mind maps and led Cranky Man into the timbered hills to the east.

He recognized a landmark and said, "We can put down here."

They made camp in the lee of a thickly timbered ridge, Fargo using crumbled bark to start a fire and bake some cornmeal-and-water balls into ash-pone.

"Wish we had some juniper wood," Cranky Man complained. "No smoke, and it smells good."

"The timber and darkness are blocking our smoke," Fargo reminded him. "Pine smoke will give our clothes the forest smell to help throw off their horses."

The two men sat around a mosquito smudge, eyes watering from the thick, damp grass smoke. A snake slithered past, rustling the tall grass near Fargo's leg. Cranky Man went for his knife, but Fargo stayed his hand.

"It's just a gopher snake," Fargo told him. "Fresh blood could alert horses. Why announce our position?"

"The horses are nervous," Cranky Man said. "They don't know what's coming, but they don't like it. Funny how a horse picks up danger signs from its rider."

Fargo, however, was in no mood for chitchat. "I think Butch Sloan is a fox-eared bastard, all right. He might have learned some trailcraft from his cousin or his outlaw adventures. I'll bet they're smart enough to desert their shack, for starters."

Cranky Man spat a bug out of his mouth. "Not to change the subject, but you saw it when we rode out of town?"

Fargo nodded. "It's better than the back-shooting jackal deserves."

"It" was the new grave for Scout Langley, rocks heaped on

it to keep scavengers away. It was dug outside the cemetery proper, unfit to be among Christians. A constant goad to the ire of the Sloan boys. . . .

"They'll try to bait us out," Fargo told Cranky Man. "I've studied this bunch. They're not toe-to-toe killers; they're dry-gulchers who fade at a fair fight. We don't know how many we're up against, so instead a letting them wear us down in a long lead-chucking contest, we'll run to their guns on the attack. They won't expect that."

"They won't—?" Cranky Man looked at Fargo, more shadow than substance in the dancing firelight. "You don't mean it?" he said, his words scorn-tipped. "They won't expect an attack into their guns? Hell, who would even suggest it but Skye damn Fargo. Why not just shoot each other right now and make it easy?"

"It'll work," Fargo said. "I've used it before. It plays to their weakness. Any man can act brave when the odds are with him—that's why this bunch favors the mass ambush. But dangerous, close-in killing ain't their dish."

"Ain't my favorite, neither. All these attacks are frazzling my nerves. Hell, I jump at every noise."

"So do they," Fargo insisted. "Criminals are used to a soft life in town. We're breaking them down."

"I'm spittin' cotton," Cranky Man groused. "Where's that giggle water you said you'd buy?"

"Sorry, old son, no strong water until we skin this last job. Drink the creek water—it's clear and cold."

Cranky Man grunted. "Yeah, it's a reg'lar tonic."

"Those pus buckets have already left this area for good or they're doing the same thing we're doing—hunting. Even if they know about Mackenzie's confession, they might decide that killing me in time saves them from prison. After all, Mackenzie's a dead man, and accused men have a right to face their accuser."

Cranky Man, who hated forced sobriety, swore out loud. "I hope our cornmeal holds out. I can't survive on berries and such—gives me the squitters."

"You done whining?" Fargo demanded. "First you ain't got the right firewood, then you're bawlin' for liquor. Now the food don't suit you. I can't be wet-nursing you, chief. Either shut up and listen for the enemy or go join the girls in their sewing lodge."

"Up yours, Fargo, with a crooked broomstick."

But Cranky Man actually fell silent and remained alert for the next half hour. Finally: "Hard to believe a man like Cody Jeffries let Felicity play him like a piano."

"He just took a freak to her," Fargo speculated. "Hell, it happens. She's a captivating woman. It was too good to be true, but he was enjoying himself too much to ask any questions."

He stood up and kicked dirt over the fire. "You turn in, and I'll take the first watch. Sleep on your weapons. We'll do turn-around every two hours. For Christ sakes, *don't* fall asleep on guard duty. Even cowards know what to do when they catch an enemy asleep."

Fargo and Cranky Man rolled out of their blankets in near darkness, brewed strong coffee and soaked hardtack in it, and were in the saddle by sunup.

Fargo began a careful patrol-and-tracking routine. In the bottoms and dry washes he often dismounted and went down on one knee.

"This bottom is all rocky," Cranky Man said. "What sign can you be reading?"

"The rocks are covered with silt," Fargo replied. "Some say a man can't track across rock, but all these disturbances in the silt tell me men with shod horses rode through here. I count four or five riders. Look here, too."

Fargo pointed to the trace-work pattern of lichen on some of the rocks. "It's been scraped off by horseshoes. And they've come this way several times."

"Patrolling for us, you mean?"

"Looks that way," Fargo said, forking leather. "Except that one of the patrollers is by himself and tracking the rest—Cody Jeffries, I'd wager. Let's be the first to find 'em and give 'em our love."

Until well after noon the two men cut plenty of sign but failed to ride down their foes. As longtime outlaws, the Sloans likely knew every escape trail and hidden cave in this part of the state. After another fruitless search of yet another brushy canyon, Cranky Man carped: "Let's take a break. Fargo, you have the endurance of a doorknob. Me, I'm what you call . . . delicate."

Fargo opened his mouth to retort, but just then the Ovaro hunkered on his hocks—a situation fraught with peril because if the hocks bent too much the horse pulled up permanently lame. Only an eyeblink later Fargo had more pressing trouble when repeating rifles opened up on them.

"Firing from the left!" he shouted. "Nerve up and run to the guns!"

As they bore down on Butch Sloan's unsavory crew, Fargo had to endure some harrowing near misses. But as he closed in to a more personal range, Henry beginning to spit fire and smoke, the outlaws realized the cat-and-mouse was over—a snarling wolverine was coming right at them, fearless and mindful only of killing.

Fargo watched all four of them disappear into a long, timbered draw. "They don't expect us to follow them into cover like that. Let's hound the sons of bitches into hell!"

They brought their mounts around into the draw, losing plenty of light. Fargo stood up in the stirrups.

"Only two riders out ahead now," he said, listening close. "I'd say the other two are a rear guard and they reined in to waylay us. Could come any time now. Keep your powder dry and your pecker hard."

Watching the good ambush points, Fargo spotted the rear guard before they spotted him and Cranky Man. They were two total strangers to him, stupid and unshaven, holed up in a tangled deadfall left of the trail. Their bright store-bought clothing gave them away.

Fargo shucked out his Colt and sent four slugs into the deadfall, raising a howl of pain. He had only tagged one of them, in the wrist. But when the wounded man ran out, howling and dancing with anguish, Fargo cut him down mercilessly.

The second man opened up on Fargo, but before the Trailsman could fire again, the crack-and-boom of the Colt Dragoon sent the man inside the deadfall into a lifeless heap, a fist-sized chunk of his torso missing. Huge gouts of blood spumed from him.

"Sorry I had to kill him," Cranky Man said. "Better to keep them alive. There's a tendon right inside the elbow bend that can be cut fast. Makes an arm useless for life. 'Course, I'd leave one good arm to wipe his ass with."

Fargo shook his head. "I say kill a man or let him go, but *don't* maim him. That's an enemy for life."

They rode for the rest of the day, but the Sloan brothers were on home range and managed to elude them. Fargo left Cranky Man at the camp and rode into town briefly to talk to Jeffries.

Fargo found him standing in front of the jailhouse, his face and clothes powdered with trail dust.

"Lester Trilby was arrested by the U.S. Marshal today," the sheriff greeted him. "I called him in because it's a federal case. Trilby spilled all he knows. Now Jonas and Baxter don't act so cocky."

"Glad to hear it," Fargo said. "I got two corpses to report."

"I found those two bodies," Jeffries told him. "Artemius thanks you and has your bonus. There's just the Sloan brothers left. They could leave this area, but they won't. That means they want you so bad they'll even give up a chance at escape."

"I'm the main chance," Fargo agreed.

"Yeah, but I couldn't find one man with the stones to swear in as deputy. So I do all the patrolling including watching their shack."

"Search it?"

Jeffries nodded. "Served a warrant but they weren't there. We found some munitions and cash buried under the shack."

He hooked a thumb toward the office. "Someone inside wants to talk to you."

Fargo considered those words a warning as he opened the jailhouse door and saw Felicity seated at the sheriff's desk. The prisoners were indeed surly but quiet. Nonetheless, Fargo led Fel back outside and around to the back of the small building.

"Skye," she said, "you didn't stay long enough for me to tell you something else. I think the gang has a final job planned. It's a bullion coach hauling gold bars to New Orleans from a bank in Saint Louis."

"Can you chew that a little finer?"

"I don't know much. It's not a military shipment. I once slipped a note from Linton to Butch Sloan about it. Linton had been tempted but decided against it—too much pure gold to get rid of. But he told me he feared that Butch couldn't resist the payoff."

"How well do you know the Sloan brothers?"

"I don't," she said with finality. "They frighten me, especially Butch. I never spoke to any of the holdup men, just passed a few notes."

"There's no connection to the army, so this bullion thing is out of my bailiwick. Do you know the date they mean to strike?"

She shook her head. Fel had dressed more modestly in a blue broadcloth skirt and crisp white shirtwaist. Her eyes suddenly welled with tears. "I don't know that because I was getting all the dates from Mack. I mean, Colonel Mackenzie. He avoided this job."

Fargo watched a tumult of misery sweep over her, but he suspected it was an act—Fel was good at deception. But she was also mighty beautiful, and a beautiful woman's crimes somehow didn't exist.

"Thanks, Fel. You sing like an angel and look like one, too."

Fel smiled bravely. "Well, every man to his fancy, right?"

Fargo nodded, astounded by her beauty and charm. She lowered her voice. "Any chance your fancy could choose me again sometime?"

"Of course," Fargo said. "Why should *I* be punished?"

Fargo and Cranky man drove their mounts hard the next day, chasing the Sloan boys from hut to hidey-hole but never getting more than a glimpse of their elusive quarry. They did, however, take the bait and draw plenty of lead, and two barrels of buckshot from a messenger gun.

"They might be cowards," Fargo said during a walk down for the horses, "but they won't give up until we end it. Let's just keep attacking."

"And before you say it," Cranky Man cut in, "let me: do we plan to live forever, right?"

By middle afternoon their horses were lathered and blowing foam. But the harassed brothers had finally lost their sneer of command as their escapes became more hairsbreadth and frantic. They had intended to play Fargo's game first, but somehow he beat them.

Two hours later a string of salty curses rang out as Butch and Romer were flushed from their latest hideout, in a rock defile, victims of the Ovaro's ear for a jingling spur.

"Good, they're in a pucker," Fargo said, reloading his Colt before he gave chase. "A hot head is a piss-poor fighter."

"That's our ace?" Cranky Man demanded. "'A hot head is a piss-poor fighter'?"

Fargo shaded his eyes from the low sun. "You best hark to the trail. All your smart-ass comments won't amount to a hill of beans if those two finally jump us. And they will—the rats are as good as cornered now and can't run unless they kill us."

But the plan was changed for them by a gunshot from a brush canyon out ahead. They rode closer, staying behind a line of willows.

Fargo saw Sheriff Cody Jeffries earning his pay the hard way. He held his six-gun on the Sloan brothers, both of whom stared at him with defiant threat.

"I see the look in your eyes, boys," Jeffries said. "I ain't looking to kill you—it's partly my fault you got away with what you did. So just ease them barking irons out real slow," he ordered, "using just two fingers."

"You're doing Fargo's bidding," Butch goaded him. "After he put the horns on you, too."

"Never mind. Just fish them out—and use only two fingers."

"Why?" Butch demanded. "So we can swing for murder? Look, Cody, throw in with us. Fargo won't look for you to kill him. Hell, he stole your woman."

"Ain't my job to kill Fargo, just to arrest—or kill—you. I prefer to take you in alive."

"Ain't our fault that pretty bitch pussy-whipped you, Jeffries," Butch replied, drawing without warning.

Jeffries was ready. He squeezed off two rounds that tore into Butch's abdomen, instantly fatal. Before Jeffries could swing his revolver, Romer raised his point-blank to kill the sheriff. Instead, Fargo, standing behind Jeffries, drilled Romer with a head shot.

"You see all of it?" the sheriff asked when he spotted Fargo.

"All the shooting part and it went by the rules. And you've still got Baxter, Jones, and Trilby to testify."

"Thanks for backing my play, Fargo. I handled it wrong—you saved my life."

"You didn't lack for guts, Sheriff."

"There's a mort of work to be done," Jeffries admitted, heaving a sigh. "But mainly it's over."

Fargo had to remain camped several days while the army processed his pay voucher and per diem claim. Federal subpoenas had been issued for him and Jeffries, both men testifying at a military tribunal. Jonas and Baxter, begging for mercy, were hanged one day later. Trilby received twenty years at hard labor, pissing himself when the judge pronounced the sentence. The name "Linton Mackenzie" no longer existed in the cavalry.

Nor did the name Felicity Meadows come up at the tribunal. Two days later, Fargo saw her being handed into an eastbound stagecoach by none other than Gilbert Daniels. The coach was full, so Daniels climbed up onto the seat behind the box. Fel stretched her neck through a window to speak to Fargo, but a shake of the reins and the six-horse stagecoach was in motion.

"What's your dicker?" Daniels called back to him, grinning.

Fargo waved his hat at them. "I'll be damned," he muttered. "The mooncalf pulled it off."

Fargo was cutting the dust at the Razorback when Lynette cozied up next to him at the bar. "You *still* think I'm a spy, Skye Fargo?"

Fargo picked her up and twirled her around, then kissed her. "No, ma'am, you're my friend."

She brought her curled blond head closer and lowered her voice. "You know that Indian you sent up? He done good in the saddle, but he ain't hardly got no damn hair on his pecker. A grown man! I like to bust a gut."

Fargo laughed. "Yeah, well you won't see too many Indians with a beard, either."

Since it was on their way, Fargo and Cranky Man paid a last visit to the Ravenels. When they rode in, Lindsay Ravenel was breaking a horse to leather. He had slipped burlap over its head so he could sneak the light breaking saddle on.

"Waste of time," Cranky Man scoffed from the saddle. "Just jump on the horse and ride him until it's blown in. If you're still on him when he stops, he's broken."

"Trouble is," Lindsay fired back, "you red sons ain't too particular whose horse you jump on."

"Not when it's for the taking," Cranky Man admitted.

Pa Ravenel heard the commotion and came outside through the kitchen door. "Skye Fargo the Mormon and Crotchety Man! Light down and eat. We're jist settin' down to vittles. Scrape the gravy skillet, Ma—we got company! Skye, you was right about them spiderwebs. Rain's been good."

This time Cranky Man made it over the muddy ditch. Fargo found Ma Ravenel dropping dumplings into a simmering pot of beans while young Cindy ground wheat in a hand gristmill. Fargo enjoyed a last home-cooked meal before he and Cranky Man said their farewells.

At the crossroad the two friends reined in.

"We square on the money?" Fargo asked.

"Square. So your needle points west?"

Fargo nodded. "I've got a job to finish out in Nebraska."

"Before you go, tell me something. Fargo, you've seen the elephant. Fought in famous battles, topped beautiful women, saved plenty more lives than you took, seen parts of this country that ain't even mapped yet—seen and done it all. Why do you keep pushing over the next ridge?"

"Just to see what's there. Appreciate it now, Cranky Man, because the howlers are going to destroy most of it. And you're wrong—no man has done it all. He can only try."

"But drifters like us can't make a fist—you know, can't succeed at something."

"Maybe so, but if I tried to roost somewhere, I'd always be dreaming of pushing on. Guess I got jackrabbits in my socks. So you're sticking around a while?"

Cranky Man nodded. "Dolomite offered me three hots and a hayloft if I work for him, so I guess I'll stay around Pine Hollow until they run me out. I'm damned if I'll go back to the rez and listen to them missionary biddies tell me all about a virgin who had a baby."

"You watch your topknot," Fargo advised. "You're a good man to ride the river with, Cranky Man. Meet you down the trail somewhere."

Fargo tugged his hat lower and gigged the Ovaro into the direction of the westering sun.

LOOKING FORWARD!
The following is the opening
section of the next novel in the exciting
Trailsman **series from Signet:**

THE TRAILSMAN #349
NEW MEXICO GUN-DOWN

New Mexico, 1861—the Sangre de Cristo Mountains,
where blood flows as freely as water.

A loud sound brought Skye Fargo out of the black pit of sleep. He sat up with a start. His first thought was that he had been shot. Pain exploded between his ears, and he winced and looked around in confusion. He was in a small room, lying on a bed, buck naked. The only other furniture was an old chest of drawers. A small tattered rug lay near the door. So did five empty whiskey bottles.

"Hell," Fargo said. He seemed to recollect drinking a lot more than he should have, which explained the pain. His mouth felt as if it was stuffed with dry wool. When he swallowed, his throat felt raw.

From beside him came the loud sound; a snore that could shake walls.

Fargo glanced down at a shapely fanny and long velvet legs and it all came back to him in a burst of memory. The fanny belonged to a dove named Amalia. Last night they had sucked down bug juice until they were both in a stupor and came to her room for a frolic under the sheets. He didn't remember much about the frolic but it must have been a dandy given how sore he was. He went to swat her backside but changed his mind. "Might as well let you sleep," he muttered.

Fargo swung his legs over the side and stood. The pounding grew worse. Smacking his dry lips, he shuffled around the bed. His buckskins and boots and gun belt were in an untidy heap. He recalled shedding them in a fit of passion and was annoyed that he hadn't kept his Colt handy. A mistake like that could cost him.

Fargo set to dressing. His body was stiff and he hurt all over, as if he'd been stomped by a bronc. He had bite marks on his arms and his lower lip was swollen. He happened to see his reflection in a mirror over the chest of drawers. "Damn," he said. His neck bore a red mark the size of an apple and there were deep scratches on both shoulders. "You're a firebrand, woman," he said with a chuckle to the still-snoring Amalia.

It took a lot longer than it should to put himself together. He was sluggish. He gave his head several hard shakes to try and clear it and regretted it when the pain became worse. Quietly opening the door, he slipped out. A window at the end of the hall was lit with the harsh glare of the New Mexico sun. His spurs jingling, he moved toward the stairs and was almost to them when someone came around the corner. They almost collided. He was looking down and all he saw was a pair of shoes and part of what he took to be a dress. "Watch where the hell you're going."

"I beg your pardon, young man."

Fargo raised his head. "Oh," he said, for lack of anything better.

It was a woman in her sixties, or older. She had more wrinkles than a prune but sparkling blue eyes and the sweetest smile this side of an angel, which was fitting since she wore a habit complete with a hood and baggy sleeves.

"I didn't mean to startle you," the nun said.

"You didn't," Fargo said more gruffly than he meant to. He went to go around her but she put a hand on his arm.

"I wonder if you could help me."

"Not now, ma'am." Fargo took a step but she held on to him.

"It's important. I'm looking for someone. Perhaps you know him."

"Lady, all I know is that I need a drink." Fargo smiled and shrugged loose and went down the stairs two at a stride. By the time he reached the bottom his head was hammering to rival a church bell. He crossed the lobby and walked out into the hot afternoon air. The bright light was so painful, he had to squint against the glare.

Las Emociones was a few doors down. Last night it had bustled with life and laughter but now only a handful of patrons were at tables and the bar. He smacked to get the barkeep's attention. "Whiskey."

The bartender was portly and friendly and wore a white cotton shirt he somehow kept spotlessly clean. He brought a bottle and said, "More, senor? If I had as much as you, I would be drunk for a week."

A few chugs and the wool was gone from Fargo's mouth. He smiled and said, "Gracias. I needed that."

"Amalia?" the bartender said.

"Passed out and trying to bring down the hotel with her snores."

The man grinned. "She will be embarrassed, senor. She likes to boast that she can drink any man under the table. In you she has finally met her match."

"I think it was a tie but I woke up first." Fargo drank more red-eye and his body shook from the jolt. The pounding was going away and he could think again.

"Do you remember everything that happened last night?" the bartender asked.

"No," Fargo admitted.

"That is too bad, senor."

"Why?"

"Because there is about to be trouble." The bartender gazed toward the entrance and bobbed his chin.

Fargo turned.

Two men were coming toward him. Both had hard dark eyes.

Both wore sombreros and pistols. They looked enough alike to be brothers. When they stopped, the tallest, and probably the oldest, put his hands on his hips, his right hand inches from his six-shooter. "Did you think we would forget you, gringo?"

For the life of him, Fargo couldn't remember either one. "Should I?"

The tall one glowered. "You imagine you are funny, yes? You treat us with contempt and think we will swallow the insult."

"Mister, I have no idea what you're talking about." Fargo went to raise the bottle and the tall one struck his arm, nearly causing him to drop it.

"No more drink for you, gringo. You have us to deal with now."

Anger flushed through Fargo's veins. He set the bottle on the bar and lowered his arms. "Who the hell *are* you?"

"I am Juan Francisco de Salas and this is my brother, Jose. You will do us the honor of stepping into the street."

"Why would I want to do that?"

"What you want doesn't matter. It is what *we* want. We were not armed last night when you knocked me down but we are armed now. You will come with us out into the street and we will settle this as men should."

Fargo looked at the bartender. "I knocked him down?"

"*Sí*, senor. They come here often. Juan is fond of Amalia. He wanted her last night but she was with you. She refused to go with him. When he tried to take her you told him to . . ." The bartender scrunched up his face. "What was it you said? Ah, yes. Now I remember. You told him to 'go fuck himself.' Juan became upset and hit you. That was when you knocked him down and his brother had to carry him out."

Fargo smiled grimly. "Well, well, well."

"The cause of the insult is not the issue," Juan said. "Now will you come with us or not?"

"Not," Fargo said, and kneed him in the groin. Juan folded over with a grunt. Fargo launched an uppercut that raised Juan onto the heels of his boots and sent him tottering against a table.

Both crashed to the floor. The brother, Jose, was rooted in disbelief. It enabled Fargo to take a quick step, streak out his Colt, and slam the barrel against Jose's temple. Both brothers were unconscious, Juan with blood trickling from his mouth, Jose with scarlet seeping from a gash in the side of his head. Fargo twirled the Colt into his holster. "Peckerwoods."

The bartender was agape. "*Caramba!* You are *rapido como el rayo*, senor. Quick as lightning."

Fargo grabbed the whiskey bottle. He slapped coins on the bar to pay for it and turned to go.

"A word, senor?" the bartender said.

Fargo stopped.

The bartender gestured at the forms on his floor. "They will not forget this. They will come after you."

"Tell them I said good luck finding me." Fargo intended to be well out of Santa Fe before the hour was up.

"They will find you, senor," the bartender said. "They are most persistent, the Salas brothers."

"It will be too bad for them if they do."

"No, senor. I am afraid it will be bad for you. They are rich, the Salas family. They have a large hacienda with many cattle and many vaqueros. Their father will not take kindly to what you have done. When he hears of it, he will send some of his vaqueros to track you down and restore the family's honor."

"Hell," Fargo said. All he'd wanted when he stopped for the night was a few drinks and a card game and a friendly dove to warm his lap.

"Or it could be the brothers will come after you themselves. It is a great insult, you beating them, and they must repay you or live in shame."

Fargo sighed.

"I only say this to warn you. I like you, senor. And it was not you who started the trouble last night."

"I'm obliged."

"What will you do?"

"Light a shuck, I reckon," Fargo said.

"Pardon, senor?"

"I don't want to kill them if I don't have to."

"If they find you, you will have to. Knocking you down would not be enough. *Comprendes*, senor?"

"Comprendo," Fargo said. To some folks, honor was worth dying over. He was about to turn and go when the bartender looked past him again and gave a slight start. Fargo spun, thinking it was more trouble.

It was the old nun. She was inside the batwings, her hands clasped at her waist, her features serene.

Everyone else stopped what they were doing to stare.

"Madre Superiora!" the bartender exclaimed, and rattled off a string of Spanish so fast, Fargo caught only half the words.

The nun came toward them, smiling. She saw the two brothers on the floor and her smile changed into a frown of disapproval. "Did you do this, senor?"

"They started it," Fargo said, and for some reason he flashed back to the time when he was eight or nine and his mother caught him and his brother fighting over an apple.

"You should not be in here, Mother Superior," the bartender said to her.

"Why not?"

The bartender gestured. "This is not the kind of place for a person like you."

"And what kind of person am I?" She touched her habit. "Under this I am just like you."

"No, you are not," the bartender said. "You are good. You are holy. This place is for the wicked."

"Oh, Carlos," she said.

The bartender blushed. "I am serious. You must leave."

"I can't," the nun said.

"Why not?"

"I must have words with him." She nodded at Fargo.

"Me?" Fargo wasn't sure he'd heard right.

"Sí, senor. Perhaps we could sit at a table and talk? It is very important. It is why I came to the hotel looking for you. But you walked off before I could explain."

"Please, Mother Superior," Carlos pleaded. "Not in here, I tell you. Go somewhere more fitting."

Juan Francisco de Salas groaned and his right hand twitched.

Fargo took that as a cue to touch his hat brim. "I'm sorry, ma'am. I have to fetch my horse and fan the breeze." He went around her and got out of there.

The livery was across the plaza. To the north of the city a high peak wore a crown of white despite it being early summer.

Fargo passed a man leading a burro and a woman carrying a large vase. No one paid attention to him. Ever since the war with Mexico and the Treaty of Guadalupe, *Norte Americanos*, as they were called, had been coming down the Santa Fe Trail in increasing numbers. Many liked the warm climate. Many liked the relaxed way of life. More than a few, notably those who lived outside the law, came to get away from the law's long reach.

The Ovaro was in the same stall where Fargo had left it. He threw on his saddle blanket and his saddle and slipped a bridle on and led the stallion out into the bright sunlight. He was raising his leg to hook his boot in the stirrup when the Salas brothers came out of the cantina. Each had a hand on his pistol. They looked about them, evidently searching, but he was on the offside of his horse and they didn't spot him. Juan said something to Jose and they moved around the edge of the plaza.

Fargo lowered his leg. Holding on to the reins, he turned in the other direction, keeping the stallion between them and him. They reached the north end as he reached the south. They turned to the west. He turned to the east. He was glad it wasn't siesta time or the plaza would be practically empty. As it was, there were enough people that he didn't stand out.

The Salas brothers reached the northwest corner. Fargo reached the southeast corner.

He could go down any of the narrow side streets but the one he wanted was near the cantina.

The brothers stopped and so did he. He watched them over the Ovaro's neck. They intently scanned the plaza, then they began to argue. Juan motioned one way and Jose the other. Finally they went the way Juan wanted and entered a side street and disappeared.

"Good riddance," Fargo said. He walked on and was almost to the cantina when the brothers came back out of the street and stood scouring passersby. Fargo swore and stopped. They were almost directly across from him. He was debating whether to climb on the stallion and use his spurs when the old nun stepped out of the cantina.

"There you are."

"Leave me be," Fargo said.

"I can't. It is too important."

"So is me getting shot."

"Ah. I see the brothers over there."

"Go away." Fargo motioned, shooing her, but she came over to the Ovaro.

"I intend to have my say."

Across the plaza, both brothers were making for the cantina.

"Oh, hell," Fargo said.

Kate Collins

The Flower Shop Mystery Series

Abby Knight is the proud owner of her hometown flower shop. She has a gift for arranging flowers—and for solving crimes.

Mum's the Word
Slay It with Flowers
Dearly Depotted
Snipped in the Bud
Acts of Violets
A Rose from the Dead
Shoots to Kill
Evil in Carnations
Sleeping with Anemone

"A sharp and funny heroine."
—Maggie Sefton

S914

GET CLUED IN

Ever wonder how to find out about all the
latest Berkley Prime Crime and
Obsidian mysteries?

berkleyobsidianmysteries.com

- See what's new
- Find author appearances
- Win fantastic prizes
- Get reading recommendations
- Sign up for the mystery newsletter
- Chat with authors and other fans
- Read interviews with authors you love

Mystery Solved.